"This isn't about us."

"It's about my brother," Clea said, denying her feelings. "It's not fair for you to desert him because you hate me. Do you want me to beg you? Or is it money? I'll pay you for your precious time."

Reeve's anger was immediate. He turned around, facing her, and grabbed her arms. "I'm not for sale, Clea, now or ever. Your father couldn't buy me off ten years ago, and *you* damn well can't buy me now."

"Let me go," she demanded.

"Oh, I'll let you go, Clea. But first you owe me something," Reeve said, while she continued to struggle. "You owe me a goodbye kiss, the one your father and the sheriff cheated me out of ten years ago."

His mouth found hers. Clea fought the kiss, till finally a great wave of acceptance came over her, and she gave in, feeling the anger drain out of her. . . . When the moment ended, memories clung between them— memories of what might have been. . . .

"Let's just say we're even, now," she murmured, breaking away from Reeve. "All debts paid." And, without looking at him again, she was gone.

Madeline Harper's sixth Temptation, *The Jade Affair*, is yet another example of this team's versatility when it comes to romance writing. Although Madeline Porter and Shannon Harper live seven states away from each other, on two different coasts (Madeline in California anb Shannon in Florida), this dynamic duo has once again created an exciting love story. Set in exotic Mexico, a favorite vacation spot for both authors, *The Jade Affair* will sweep you away!

This team also writes under the name Anna James.

Books by Madeline Harper

HARLEQUIN TEMPTATION

The Jade Affair
MADELINE HARPER

Harlequin Books

TORONTO • NEW YORK • LONDON
AMSTERDAM • PARIS • SYDNEY • HAMBURG
STOCKHOLM • ATHENS • TOKYO • MILAN

Published December 1990

ISBN 0-373-25426-1

THE JADE AFFAIR

Prologue

THE SMALL COTTAGE was on a deserted stretch of beach near Monterey. Hidden from the road behind a spindly stand of pine trees, it looked out on pebble-strewn sand washed by the Pacific.

The afternoon sun hovered near the horizon, bathing the two young people who emerged from the sea in its rosy glow. She was long-legged and slim; her blond hair hung wet and sleek against her shoulders. He was dark and stockily muscular in build. He encircled her waist with his arm in a proprietary and protective way.

"You're a water nymph," he said, giving her a salty kiss as they made their way across the beach. "You outraced me again."

"I like to win," she replied, dashing ahead of him toward the cottage.

He followed her, reaching for a towel as they burst through the door. As he dried her hair he said, "And I like *you*." He punctuated his words with a kiss. "I like this weekend, this cottage, and I even like Charlie because he found it for us."

She stood quietly like an obedient child, letting him dry her, luxuriating in the touch of the rough terry cloth against her cool skin. "Big brothers are sometimes useful."

"Yeah, Charlie can be a great guy as well as a pain in the . . . neck."

"He brought us together," she countered with her gamine's grin.

"Like I said, he's a really, really great guy." Laughing softly, he dropped the towel, reached for her and carried her to the bed. She was warm and sweet in his arms, and he held her close, feeling her flesh merge into his. Through the thin fabric of her suit he could feel the curve of her young breasts, the taut, budding nipples pressed against him. A little tremor played through his own tight muscles.

"Oh, Clea, I love you so."

"And I love you, my darling Reeve." She raised her face, as fresh as a spring flower, to his, and he drank from her lips in a long, deep kiss. She let her mouth drift away from his, along the curve of his chin, his strong neck, the muscles of his shoulders.

He moved his hands slowly up her arms, all the while watching the expression on her upturned face. "How could you possibly love *me*, a guy from nowhere with a hell of a past and not much of a future?"

Color flamed her cheeks. "Because you're wonderful, Reeve Holden! You're the most wonderful man in the world, and I don't care what anyone says—not even my parents. I don't care about anything but you." She was in love for the first time in her life, and it was a love as pure as the sand that shifted on the beach, as honest as the expression on her glowing face.

"How did I ever get so lucky?" he asked, and this time he didn't wait for an answer as he kissed her deeply, thoroughly. He found the silken recesses of her mouth with his tongue, tasting the saltiness there. He could hear the wild pounding of his heart and feel the blood racing through his veins. Her body was a bright flame burning hot against him. He was ignited by her touch.

"Oh, my Clea, do you know how much I want you?" His voice was husky with desire.

In answer, she took his hand and raised it to her breast. He felt the warmth of her skin, and it suffused him with a fire brighter than the setting sun. Slowly he moved his hand to the straps of her suit and slipped them from her shoulders. Now his lips could touch her breast, taste its rosy bud.

He slid the suit down and in less than a moment she was naked before him, waiting, arms outstretched.

"Oh, Clea . . ." His voice seemed strangled, muted. "I'll love you forever, until the day I die."

"I'll never love another man, Reeve. Never." She reached for him and drew him down on the bed beside her, feeling the heat of his body against hers. She helped him pull off his bathing suit then she touched his manhood, held him in her trembling hands, excited and yet tentative, too, because it was all so new to her.

Time stood still for a moment while her heart pounded so fiercely that she was sure it would burst. She wanted to tell him so much, so much, but there was no way to put her feelings into words. There was only Reeve and his body hard against hers and the need inside her that curled and twisted and made her cry out.

He turned her in his arms then moved slowly, carefully, until he was above her. Opening her legs gently with his hands he lowered himself down. She felt his weight heavy on her, felt his manhood at that place where her need was greatest. Then time rushed forward and he was inside her welcoming body where she was warm and moist and ready for him.

Clea clung tightly, her arms around his strong, damp back, and they moved together, their tanned young bodies in perfect harmony. She wrapped her legs around him instinctively, pulling him closer, and he responded with all the passion he possessed until she felt herself carried away on a tide of love and pleasure that she had never imagined could exist.

"ARE YOU ALL RIGHT?" His voice was soft, his touch gentle on her skin.

"I'm wonderful," she said and then, giggling, added, "I mean I *feel* wonderful." She snuggled close against him. "I never want this night to end, ever."

Reeve felt his heart fill with love. There was so much he wanted to say to her that his words came out with a rush. "I loved you from the first time I saw you. Do you remember, Clea, when Charlie brought me to your house on Thanksgiving?"

"I remember." She did, fervently. She remembered the first moment they met, the first look they shared, the first touch.

Reeve remembered, too, but he didn't say how out of place he'd felt as a lowly Naval ensign brought to the wealthy Moore mansion in Beverly Hills. That's where he'd first seen Clea. She was blond and beautiful, gracious and lovely, as friendly as her parents were cool and distant. There was no doubt that from the beginning the elder Moores believed he wasn't half good enough for their daughter.

Then, miracle of miracles, Reeve found out that Clea loved him, too. In his awed reaction to her love, there existed the fear of losing her. He never voiced that fear, because just saying it might bring it to pass.

"You were so handsome in your uniform," she said. "Remember the picture I took, pretending I wanted Charlie in his dress whites? 'Course, what I really wanted was a photograph of you, one to keep. I was like a silly schoolgirl."

"You're so old now," he teased.

"Almost eighteen," she said defiantly, "and you're only twenty-one. That hardly makes you an old man!"

"Twenty-one *is* a man, Clea. Old enough to vote and..." He paused and took a deep breath. "Old enough to get married. Oh, Clea, I want to marry you."

She was in his arms in an instant, raining kisses along his chin and cheek. "And I want to marry you, more than anything." She lay across him, her face inches from his, her hair hanging loose like a golden screen.

"When I get out of the Navy, I'll buy a boat," he said, his voice boyish with enthusiasm. "We'll sail the world together, just you and me, Clea." He was making all kinds of plans now, spinning them from his dreams, and she was trying to keep up with him.

Inside, Clea was in turmoil. She tried to separate reason from emotion, but she couldn't. Her love for Reeve was too great. Tentatively she reminded him, "We'd have to run away."

"Yes," he whispered.

"My parents would never approve, not now...."

He held her hand in his, tightly. "Not now or ever, but this is us, Clea, you and me, not your parents. If we love each other, then we have to do this right away or we never will. We could lose everything."

She sat up, a frown creasing her forehead. "If we can just make them understand how much we love each other—"

"Clea," he said, shaking her lightly, "your parents will never be understanding about me. You know that."

She disagreed in her mind, but in her heart she was afraid that what Reeve said was true.

"We need to get married right away. This weekend."

"I want to marry you, Reeve, I do—" she hesitated again "—but I still think it would be better if we waited, not for years, just until I finish school. They would never forgive me if we ran away."

He turned to her then. "I know."

Clea had to fight back the tears that were close to the surface. "What's happening?" she cried. "This was the most wonderful night of my life, and now you're trying to ruin it."

Reeve swung his feet onto the floor and stood up. She could see that he was fighting to stay in control. "You're going to have to choose, Clea."

"I don't want to hurt them, Reeve."

"But it's all right to hurt me?"

"No, I love you more than anything in the world. But I love them, too. Oh, why does it have to be so difficult?" she cried.

"Because they won't let us be. You know that, don't you?"

She never had a chance to answer.

The sound of knocking at the door brought an end to everything. It was loud and invasive, and intuitively they seemed to know what it meant.

"I have to answer it," Reeve said, his voice wooden as he walked to the door.

Clea wrapped herself in the sheet and scrambled to the far end of the bed, feeling lonely and very fright-

ened as she heard the deep male voice sound a warning.

"Sheriff's department, young man. We got word of
a runaway here, and we've come to pick her up."

1

CLEA MOORE DROPPED her camera bag, tripod and light stands inside the studio and pushed them aside so she could close the door. The rest of her equipment would have to stay in the car overnight; she was too exhausted to lug it another step. It had been a crazy day.

Pulling the door to, Clea brushed a strand of pale blond hair out of her eyes and took a deep breath, the first free and easy one in hours. She locked the studio and climbed the stairs that clung to the outside of her two-story frame house.

Even though it was a little rickety, Clea still considered hers one of the most charming houses in the beach town of Venice, California. It offered the convenience of a downstairs studio and upstairs living quarters, and it was located at the far end of the boardwalk, away from the summer crowds.

There was a breeze coming off the ocean, and the jasmine smelled especially delicious in the cool, clear night air. It was almost enough to put the day's photo shoot out of her mind.

Almost—but not quite. It had been a near disaster— what with the model complaining about her wardrobe, the client complaining about the model, and the makeup man complaining about everyone then pouting in the corner over his love life, or lack of it.

If she came away from that menagerie with any good shots, she deserved some kind of medal, Clea decided.

But she had to be rational about it. *It's your job, you get paid well, and no one is forcing you to do it.* "Besides, this is what you always wanted, right?" she asked herself aloud, as she opened the door to her upstairs apartment and headed for the answering machine.

"Hi, Clea. It's Penny from *Trends* magazine," said the first message. "We need you for a shoot next Tuesday. Pencil in the entire morning if you can. It's a layout of a home in Bel Air; you know the kind of thing—lots of style and gracious living. Get back to me before tomorrow, please."

Clea grimaced and pulled out her appointment book. She knew the kind of thing, all right.

"Clea, this is Dad," came the next message. "Haven't heard from you this week. Give Mom or me a call." Clea smiled at that one. After twenty-seven years, her parents still worried if she didn't check in every day or two.

Clea riffled through her mail as she listened to the next few messages. Then she heard a voice that made her stop and look up, her senses sharpened.

"Hey, Sis. The prodigal brother surfaces. I bet you got my card, huh? Well, I'm still down here in Santa Inez and things are a little more serious than I let on. So be a pal and get hold of Reeve for me. I've been trying to reach him for more than a week, and it's not about the good fishing I mentioned before; I need his help, Clea. I'm counting on you to find him."

That was the end of the tape. Clea rewound it and played her brother's message once more. As she listened, she rummaged through stacks of old mail and found the postcard she'd received a few days before and summarily dismissed.

It was postmarked Santa Inez, on the Baja peninsula in Mexico, and it was one of those wish-you-were-here cards with a casual P.S. "See if you can reach Reeve Holden for me and tell him to come on down. The fishing's great."

She should have known when she got the card that there was more at stake than *fishing*. Charlie was in trouble again. It seemed to follow after him like a dark cloud that couldn't be dispersed. In fact, Charlie never had grown up. He went from scheme to scheme, always on the edge of a fortune, but never quite there. Careless, unpredictable, irresponsible, charming—all those attributes, not to mention his abundance of nerve, described Charlie quite well.

His most recent request must have taken a great deal of gall, indeed. Or insensitivity. Clea glanced at the postcard again. "See if you can reach Reeve Holden for me. . . ."

Surely he knew that she would never act on that casual request. So he'd waited a few days then called with a more urgent message.

Clea's brown eyes darkened at the unavoidable memory of Reeve, and she shook her head as if to dislodge the pain of it. It had been almost ten years since she'd last seen Reeve, ten years since that never-to-be-forgotten summer.

Clea put the postcard away and went into the kitchen to heat up something for dinner. But she never got around to it. Reeve was in the way.

Over the years, Charlie had maintained his friendship with Reeve in the same careless way he did with others. Whenever he'd mentioned Reeve, Clea had pretended to be disinterested even though she longed to hear about him. Reeve had married; that much she

knew. Somewhere along the way he'd moved to Newport Beach, bought a boat called the *Argosy* and started
a charter service.

Since they'd gone their separate ways, she'd never
seen him, never heard from him even though they were
barely an hour's drive from each other.

Without even thinking about what she was doing,
Clea went into the living room and opened the hall
closet. There it was on the top shelf—the photograph
album she'd never quite gotten around to packing away.

She took it down, blew off the dust and opened it to
the first page.

She and Reeve and Charlie stood on the green lawn
of her parents' house. The boys wore dress whites, and
Clea was in a yellow outfit that perfectly suited the celebration of Charlie's twenty-first birthday. She and
Charlie had an air of moneyed style about them even
then, both slim and blond and patrician.

And there was Reeve with his dark hair and muscular body, a little uncomfortable and out of place on
the manicured lawn beside the Moores' swimming
pool.

Clea gently touched the photograph. They'd all been
so young—she seventeen and Reeve barely twenty-one.
They'd been so much in love. There was no love like
first love, supposedly. It was certainly true for Clea,
considering the happiness she'd felt that one and only
time—and the hurt that had followed. Since, she'd
vowed Reeve was a part of the past and should stay that
way.

Yet now that would be impossible. Charlie was in
trouble, and Clea knew that she would do as he wished
and find Reeve in spite of her feelings. Certainly Charlie hadn't considered the awkwardness of the situation

when he'd asked this favor of her. Returning the album to the shelf, Clea sighed deeply and wished to heaven Charlie had never put her in this position.

BUSINESS AT THE STUFT SAILOR Bar and Grill was slow. Pokey Barstow, the owner and bartender, had plenty of time to stop and talk, but his customer didn't seem interested.

"So this guy's been calling you from Mexico almost every day."

Reeve Holden glanced nonchalantly at the messages Pokey handed him. "Looks like it. Pass the salsa, Pokey; these eggs need all the help they can get."

"Whataya talking?" Pokey said. "We got the best *huevos rancheros* this side of Tijuana."

Reeve grunted noncommittally and poured on the salsa.

"You not even gonna call this Charlie fellow back?"

When Reeve didn't respond, Pokey continued. Reeve had long ago surmised that Pokey, being a bartender, was used to hearing the sound of his own philosophizing voice. Responses weren't needed.

"I don't get you, Reeve. The guy's been calling the whole time you were out on your charter."

"He always was persistent," Reeve responded. "How about a refill on this coffee?"

Pokey obliged but didn't let up on his questions. "So you know this feller, huh? Well, what is he, some rich guy wanting a charter and you're passing it by?"

"Not by a long shot. You think there's some intrigue going on, don't you, Pokey."

"Maybe. We could use a little excitement."

"Well, let me assure you, Charlie's kind of excitement you can get anywhere. He was a friend a long time

ago, though why I can't imagine since all he had to offer was trouble. If I know him, Charlie's probably being
chased by a jealous husband. His kind of excitement
rarely rises above that level, and I've outgrown riding
to ol' Charlie Moore's rescue."

"Good friends are hard to find," Pokey elicited.

"No argument there," Reeve replied, reaching for the
check. "Hey, Poke, add a six-pack of beer to this, would
you? My last clients cleaned out the refrigerator."

Pokey obliged, but as Reeve paid and picked up the
beer, he made one last try to satisfy his curiosity. "So
how'd the guy know he could reach you here?"

Reeve shrugged. "Everybody knows this is my home
away from home, even ol' Charlie. He may be a con-
niver, but he's far from dumb."

"So if he calls again, should I give him your ship to
shore radio? What should I tell him?"

"If he calls again, tell him I'm off to Tahiti."

Reeve walked along the street to the dock, the six-
pack swinging at his side. It had been a good cruise—
a nice, solid week's charter with three avid fishermen.
They'd hauled in a better than average catch and added
a fat bonus to his fee. All in all, a successful week.

Reeve ducked through a narrow walkway and onto
the marina. It was late. All of the trendy restaurants
along the waterfront had closed, and only a few people
remained, cleaning tables, sweeping sidewalks, pre-
paring for another day.

He stopped near the end of the wharf and looked
across at the *Argosy*. She was a beautiful thirty-six-foot
sloop that could go under sail as well as power—a
dream come true.

He'd bought her on a hunch—the kind of inspiration that came around once in a lifetime and nudged a

man to act on gut instinct. That was the *Argosy*. As he went aboard, Reeve remembered exactly how it had happened to him.

After his divorce, he'd quit a perfectly good job and spent an inordinate amount of time lounging around, thinking about what he really wanted to do. With no ties, no family, no responsibility, Reeve easily could have turned into a beach bum.

Something in his nature prevented that. Whether it was his affinity for hard work or his love of the sea or both, Reeve only knew that fate directed him to Dana Point that spring day just as the *Argosy* put in to port.

She was for sale, but Reeve was thousands of dollars short of the asking price. Later that day he had a few beers with Charlie at the Stuft Sailor and mentioned how much he wanted the boat, expressing his regrets over not being able to buy the *Argosy*.

The next day Charlie showed up with a check. Reeve argued; Charlie insisted.

"It's only money, pal, and you'll pay me back."

Even though the *Argosy* loan had been paid off with interest—and Charlie had even made money on it—Reeve never forgot how his friend had come through.

But trouble seemed to follow Charlie around, and every couple of years when the trouble got really heavy he turned to Reeve. After the last big mess, Reeve had decided that enough was enough. Now Charlie was back, but Reeve was ready to call it quits.

He opened a beer and walked to the prow where he could look out over the bay. It wasn't just the call from Charlie that was getting to him. It was all the memories that call dredged up. It was Clea.

The last time Charlie had been around he'd brought news that Clea was engaged. She'd be married by now,

Reeve assumed. Knowing that, he ought to be able to forget her, but it wasn't that easy.

They lived in close proximity, and he used to imagine they'd run into each other one day. That never happened, and he finally realized it never would. He and Clea didn't travel in the same circles. She was strictly champagne, caviar and limos; he was beer, pretzels and pickup trucks.

"It's just as well," Reeve said to himself. "We never could have made it. Sometimes love just isn't enough."

CLEA HADN'T EXPECTED to be so nervous as she pulled into the Newport Marina parking lot.

She didn't know how to reach Reeve. She only knew that he had a boat at the Newport Marina, and she'd gambled that he'd be there. Besides, if she'd called, he might have shunned her. Clea couldn't have handled that, not after all those years. Anyway this was for Charlie, and she needed to state her case without any extraneous problems to confuse the issue.

Slowly she got out of the car and walked along the marina toward the *Argosy.* Reeve's boat . . .

It was beautiful. Freshly painted, with wood highly polished and brass shining, the *Argosy* lay at dock, white and gleaming in the morning sun. She stood looking at the boat, too nervous to step aboard.

Then she saw Reeve. He was bent over the engine, and as he tinkered, he stopped occasionally to wipe his hands on a towel hanging on the railing. He'd taken off his shirt, and she could see the play of long, lean muscles as he struggled with the wrench.

Tanned, fit and healthy, he looked just as she imagined he would, and the sight of him brought back memories of his strength—and his gentleness.

He straightened up to face her just as she spoke his name.

"Reeve..." It sounded high and shrill, and she couldn't seem to get enough air in her lungs for that one syllable.

He looked at her, silently, and didn't move. He seemed prepared for her. It was as if something indefinable was there between them, waiting.

"Clea, what the hell—?"

The look of surprise on his face came too late. Clea knew he *had* been waiting for her. "It's about Charlie," she said, and for a brief moment Clea thought she saw disappointment in his look.

Then the moment was over, and his expression changed to disdain. "Oh, yeah, big brother's in trouble again and needs to be bailed out." He picked up the T-shirt that hung over the railing and pulled it over his head. The movement tousled his dark hair, which he brushed back with an impatient hand. It was a gesture so familiar, so intimate and real, that she felt a sudden painful lurch in her stomach.

"He's been trying to get in touch with you," she said, relieved that her voice sounded more natural now.

"Yeah, I know." Reeve's deep blue eyes reflected nothing more than wariness and disinterest. "My days of getting your brother out of trouble are over, Clea. I came to his aid for years, but that's all behind me now."

Whatever else he meant, she understood one thing: a great deal of time had passed for all of them. Yet the years had been kind to Reeve. He was still trim but more muscled now. Heavier and harder, he had the look of a boxer in his prime, a fighter ready to face any opponent.

His dark hair was longer than it had been once, and his face had lost its youthful fullness and was replaced with a striking angular look, accentuated by his high cheekbones and straight, dark brows. His eyes had not changed; they were still that incredible shade of blue, but they now watched her with a measure of cynicism and hardness she didn't know Reeve possessed.

Clea felt the need to explain herself. "I had to ask, Reeve," she said softly. "Charlie wanted me to."

"Sure, Clea," he responded, picking up the towel and getting the last of the grease off his hands.

He'd missed a smudge on his cheek, though, and Clea fought the urge to step onto the boat and wipe it away for him.

"I understand that," he said in a voice that was almost kind. "I remember your feelings about family."

Clea knew what was coming.

"Their wishes always came first," he added, proving Clea right.

She didn't answer; there *was* no easy explanation for the Moore family.

"But I'm forgetting my manners," he said quickly. "Come on aboard and down to the cabin while I wash up, and then we can have a beer. After all, you've driven a long way..." He stopped and looked at her with a smile. "Oh, yeah. I remember. You don't like beer. It's champagne, isn't it?"

"That's not exactly true," she responded.

"Oh? Things have changed?" He was baiting her, trying to make her feel uncomfortable. She really didn't blame him, especially after the way it had ended between them.

"Actually, *I've* changed," she was pleased to tell him. "I like beer. And champagne," she added. "But it's too early for either."

"You have a point there," he admitted, "but come down anyway while I wash up. We'll find something to refresh you."

For a moment Clea thought of declining but changed her mind. She wanted to see his boat so she followed him, silently.

While Reeve ducked away to clean up, she took the time to look around. The cabin was neat and clean, just like the rest of the boat, with shining brass and wood and glass, but there was a kind of homeyness, too. The bookcases were filled with books that looked well read and the walls hung with paintings that she knew Reeve had chosen. There'd been no decorator here; it was all Reeve and very attractive. Despite her misgivings, Clea was glad she'd come.

Noting her interest when he returned to the cabin, Reeve explained, "There're two other cabins, enough room for charters."

"It's perfect," she said.

He didn't seem ready to accept that; his defenses were still up. "But not to be compared with your home place, of course."

Clea was determined not to respond. She was almost glad for his cynicism; it replaced the spell she had begun to fall under.

Reeve smiled, seemingly aware of the change in mood. "Since you declined the beer, what about a cup of coffee?" he offered. "There's a pot brewing in the galley."

"No, I—I'm fine," she said, recovering her composure, but Clea still wasn't sure she'd be able to hold a cup without her hand shaking.

He stood still, looking at her; she returned his look in a moment of speechlessness that was anything but companionable. It was time for her to leave. She'd seen his boat and admired it, and he'd deflected her compliments as if he didn't care. She'd asked him to help, and he'd refused. There was nothing else to say, no reason to stay here. Yet she didn't move, looking at him as he looked at her, unsure what to do next.

"So why don't you sit down, Clea?" he asked finally, motioning her to the captain's chair nearby. "The last time I saw Charlie he said you had your own studio." He leaned back in his own chair, looking totally in control.

"That's right. I do. It's done very well, as a matter of fact." For some reason Clea felt the need to assert herself.

"I'm sure of that," Reeve agreed. "You always were a fine photographer. What kind of stuff are you doing now? I was thinking about a new brochure for my charter business."

She had a feeling he was baiting her again, but she didn't care. Her work was good, whatever the subject matter. "I specialize in fashion."

Reeve raised an eyebrow. "Glitz and glamour, eh? The world the Moores know and love . . ."

She didn't miss the sarcasm, but she decided to tell it all and let him scoff. "Occasionally I do parties, social events, and recently I've shot some homes. . . ."

"Architectural photos?"

"No, actually. More life-styles . . ."

"Of the rich and famous," he finished. "In that case, your family's connections must have come in handy."

"Not really, I—"

"Come now, Clea," he insisted. "We both know what can be accomplished with powerful connections."

Clea's mind flashed back to a time when her family's connections had done so much damage, had ruined everything for her and Reeve, and she felt tears burning her eyes, but she forced herself to respond calmly.

"I admit some doors have been opened for me, but I've worked hard and gotten where I am because I'm good." Clea wasn't bragging; she just wanted to regain some semblance of control.

"We've both done pretty well for ourselves, I guess," she continued, shifting in the chair to look around. "You could live here all the time."

"I do live here all the time, Clea. The *Argosy* is my home."

"What about your family?" She knew the question was awkwardly framed, but she needed to know.

"Family?" He looked genuinely puzzled. "My parents aren't living, Clea. You know that."

"I was talking about your wife." Why was it so painful to say the word?

"You mean my ex-wife. I've been divorced for three years. She's happily remarried and living in Seattle."

"Oh, I'm sorry," Clea said for lack of a better response.

"Don't be. It just didn't work out."

She almost said *I'm sorry* again but caught herself in time and remained silent while she tried to think of another reply.

"What about you?" he asked suddenly, softly.

"I—not much, just my work."

"Charlie said you were engaged."

"We broke it off."

"What happened, your dad didn't approve?"

Clea felt herself flinch but recovered quickly. "No, my parents both liked him very much. More than I did, as it turned out."

Reeve smiled. "Maybe you didn't take enough time to get to know him."

"He was an old family friend. We probably knew each other too well, actually."

"Not like us," Reeve reminded her. "Two kids from different worlds who didn't know each other at all. Lightning bolts, eh?"

Before she could speak he went on with a bitter smile. "I guess I had to learn that lightning can burn." His eyes bored into her, and he could see the flush that suffused her face.

"Then it's good that lightning doesn't strike twice in the same place," Clea said fighting the tremor in her voice.

"I hope that's true." It was a fervent hope because Reeve knew that he could get caught up in her again. Nothing about her had changed. She still wore the same perfume. Its scent, light and heady, enveloped him. She was still as beautiful as the first time he'd set eyes on her. Her thick blond hair wasn't hanging loose the way it used to, though. She'd pulled it back with a clip at the nape of her neck, revealing all the loveliness of that well-remembered face and dark, dark eyes that gave her blond beauty such exoticism.

She was wearing white linen pants and a bright turquoise silk blouse with gold loop earrings and a gold chain around her neck—all real, he knew. She looked elegant and classy and expensive. But she looked much more than that, and she always had. The years faded away, and once more she mesmerized him.

"So what kind of trouble is Charlie into now?" he asked, trying to break the spell.

"That's just the problem. I don't now. He didn't leave me a number where I could reach him in Santa Inez, the town on Baja he called from."

Reeve nodded without mentioning that he had the number.

"I spent most of last night with the long distance operator calling hotels in the area," Clea continued. "I found one where he'd been registered one day and checked out the next. I haven't heard from him again, and I'm really worried this time."

"Charlie can take care of himself."

"No, he can't," Clea argued. "He has a nose for trouble, Reeve, as you well know."

"And he'll never learn as long as someone always comes along to bail him out. You and your parents have spoiled him."

"You were guilty of that, too," Clea reminded Reeve. "There were plenty of times you stood up for my brother. Remember when those men jumped him in the bar?"

"Which bar, which time?" Reeve gibed. "He seemed to have a penchant for trying to buy a girl a drink and then learning there was a very jealous boyfriend lurking in the background. His bad luck was legendary."

"But you always dove in, didn't you, got Charlie out of the scrape and brought him home?"

"To dirty looks from your parents who were sure I'd lured their precious son to lowlife sailor haunts. If they'd only known I was usually there to drag him out . . ."

Clea smiled fondly. "There's something about Charlie that makes people want to take care of him."

"Boyish charm wears thin, Clea. I grew up; Charlie didn't."

Clea tried to argue, but Reeve cut her short. "Let me give you an example. Two years ago I got a frantic call around two in the morning. It was Charlie. He'd made a terrific deal with some night club for T-shirts silk-screened with a hot group they were promoting. He had the logo—one of a kind, original, terrific. He sold the guys on it, but the trouble was he didn't have anyone to print the shirts. The club wanted delivery right away. So Charlie called me. After checking around he found a factory out near the desert to do the silk-screening. Like a jerk, I drove Charlie out there and waited around while they printed the shirts."

Clea started to interrupt, but he stopped her. "When we got back to the club and began unloading, Charlie got into an argument with the owners. They didn't like the ink color and were trying to refuse the order. Your brother told them I was a hit man and would break their legs if they didn't pay up."

Clea bit back a smile. "That sounds like vintage Charlie."

Reeve threw her a sharp look, answering, "I didn't find it that amusing, Clea. Charlie got his money, and he thought the whole episode was a lark. As for me, I was surprised the guys didn't follow us and blow up my boat. I'm tired of being on the receiving end of Charlie's lies, and I'm too damned old for any more adventures. Period."

That fact established, Reeve changed the subject. "It's time for coffee. Sure you don't want any?"

"I'm sure."

Reeve went to the galley and returned with a mug in his hand.

"I understand how you feel, Reeve, but this time I'm really worried about him."

"Then call the local police, and let them track him down." Seeing the sudden wary look in Clea's eyes, he added, "Or maybe you don't want the police involved. One never knows with old Charlie."

Clea flushed. "I'm sure he's not in that kind of trouble." But her voice didn't reflect her supposed surety.

"*What* kind of business is Charlie in these days? It was land development last time we talked and some scheme to patent computer programs before that. Then of course there was his notable T-shirt career."

"Import-export," she answered a little hesitantly. "That's why he's in Mexico."

Reeve raised a skeptical eyebrow. "Import-export. Lots of possibilities there."

"I'm sure there's nothing illegal," she insisted. "I'm also sure that something is seriously wrong."

"Then fly down if you're so concerned. Mexico is beautiful at this time of year."

"I might," Clea decided, "but he specifically asked for you, Reeve. He wouldn't do that unless he really needed you."

"Sorry, I'm not available." His answer was cold and abrupt.

"That's all you have to say after ten years of friendship—you're not *available?*"

"Weren't you listening, Clea? I just told you what it's been like with your brother. I'm not bailing him out again, and I don't want to be caught up in his tangle of lies."

His words were intentionally cruel to counteract the golden web that he felt was drawing him in again, the glittering charm of the Moores. He had to fight it.

"You have a short memory, Reeve Holden. Charlie was your best friend; he would have walked on hot coals for you. He thought you were the greatest...."

"When he needed me," Reeve broke in harshly.

"That's not true," she argued. "He was loyal to you always, and he believed in *us*."

"Much more than you did, Clea." It was all coming back in waves of pain and passion, and Reeve could no longer contain his anger.

"This isn't about us; it's about Charlie, and it's not fair for you to desert him because you hate me. Do you want me to beg you? Is that what you want?" Her voice trembled in anger. "Or is it money? All right, I'll pay you for your precious time."

The moment Clea spoke she realized her mistake. His anger was immediate. He surged across the room and grabbed her arm, pulling her out of the chair. "I'm not for sale, Clea, now or ever. Your father couldn't buy me off ten years ago, and you damned well can't buy me now."

Clea had seen him this way only once before, and it frightened her. She tried to twist from his grip. "I didn't mean it like that."

"Your kind never do," he replied bitterly. "The bottom line is that I'm not going to Mexico, and I'm through with the Moores." Holding both her arms below the shoulders, he gave her a shake. "Understand?"

Clea's eyes blazed, and her voice trembled. "Oh, I understand all right. Your anger at me has made you forget about your friendship with Charlie. What about loyalty, Reeve?"

"You're a fine one to talk about loyalty, Clea."

They stood glaring at each other, her arms still pinioned by his hands. Their breaths were rasping, their faces flushed with anger. She tried to pull away again, but he held her fast. She could hear the dual pounding of their hearts and feel the blood rushing through her veins.

"Let me go," she demanded. "There's nothing more for us to say, and I want to get out of here."

"Oh, I'll let you go, Clea. I wouldn't want to hold you against your will. But first you owe me something."

Clea continued to struggle, but his hands were like steel vises, containing her totally.

"You owe me a goodbye kiss, the one your father and the sheriff cheated me out of ten years ago." His arms closed around her, pulling her close while she continued to struggle, uselessly.

Clea managed to turn her head away as his face came closer, but still holding her with one arm he grabbed her chin and forced her to look at him. His large hand held her face, and his eyes blazed into hers for a long moment before his mouth found hers. It was hard and demanding.

Clea fought the kiss as she'd fought Reeve, squirming in his grasp, pushing against his chest. Then something came over her, a great wave of acceptance that caused the battle to ease. Her mouth opened under his invading tongue, and Clea gave herself to the kiss, responding with a passion that equaled his.

They remained locked together, their lips bruising each other, their bodies bound in need and desire.

When the kiss ended, Clea buried her face against his shoulder. The anger was gone, drained from both of them, but the pain of memory remained. She drew in deep gulps of air and fought for control.

"Clea . . ." He dropped his arms and stepped back, as stunned as Clea by what had happened. "I never meant . . ."

His movement away from her gave Clea the space she needed. "It's all right, Reeve. It doesn't matter." Frantically, she looked around for her purse and picked it up with trembling hands. She had to leave, to run as fast as she could, not only from the memories but from the emotions his kiss had aroused in her. At the door she turned and faced him, voice shaking, fighting back her tears. "Let's just say we're even now. All debts paid."

Then, without looking at him again, she was gone.

2

"DAMN, DAMN, DAMN." The words echoed across the bay as Reeve headed toward his cabin. He felt as if he'd been hit in the solar plexus with a giant fist. How could just seeing her affect him this way after so many years?

He was a seasoned adult now, Reeve reminded himself, not a young man caught in the throes of first love. He was successful, confident, self-sufficient, but less than half an hour with Clea and all those attributes were reduced to nothing. He became as helpless as he'd been the day she'd walked into his life—or rather when Charlie took him on his first visit to the Moore estate. He would never forget the day he'd met her—or the terrible night at the little cottage in Monterey when he'd lost her.

They'd just been kids, and they hadn't deserved what had happened to them—the humiliation, the hurt, the bitterness.

Clea had been whisked away, back to her parents, and Reeve had cooled his heels for twelve hours in the local jail. After a sleepless night, he'd had a visitor, not an unexpected one.

Charles H. Moore, Sr., was in his mid-forties then. Slim and blond, he was a sportsman with trophies to prove it in tennis, golf and yachting. His tailor-made suit and perfectly trimmed hair was in direct contrast to Reeve's rumpled shirt and trousers and his Navy is-sue haircut.

Moore's first words were an order. "Sit down, young man. We've got a lot of talking to do."

"Thank you, but I prefer to stand. Sir."

"Suit yourself." Moore dropped into a straight-backed chair and waved the guard away out of earshot. "Are you concerned about being AWOL, boy?"

Reeve flinched at the word *boy*. "It doesn't really matter, sir."

"Well, it might later, but don't worry. It's taken care of. I made a phone call to one of my old friends at the Pentagon, who passed the word down. You're excused until tonight."

Reeve refused to thank him. "It pays to know people in high places, but right now I don't care about the Navy. What I care about is Clea. Is she all right?"

"My daughter is fine." The older man's voice was clipped and cold.

"I want to see her. I need to know—"

"You need to know nothing."

Reeve started toward his adversary. "Tell me where she is," he demanded.

"I see no harm in telling you that." Moore glanced at his gold pocket watch. "At the moment she's on a plane to Switzerland. She'll be in school there for a while."

"Until I'm out of the picture?"

"You're a smart boy, Holden."

"I'll never be out of the picture," he vowed emotionally.

Moore sized him up with cold blue eyes. "You know, Holden, even though you're not the man for my daughter, you have spunk. And you've come a long way from your unfortunate beginnings."

"I suppose you've had detectives checking me out."

"Precisely. From the first moment I knew Clea was interested. Let's see." Moore closed his eyes as he tried to recall the Holden dossier. "Born to Margaret Holden in a small town near Boston. Never knew your father. Grew up on the docks. Made it through school although you didn't care much for your studies. After your mother died, you joined the Navy. In spite of your less than outstanding academic record, you were considered a bright kid, a go-getter. You've done well, I'm told."

"Thanks for the bio, but I'm aware of my past."

"Past is past, my boy, but I can help secure your future."

"I don't want your help," Reeve said stubbornly.

"Don't be so damned hasty. You haven't even heard my proposal." Moore pulled out his checkbook. "I can give you more money than you'll make in a lifetime, and all you have to do in return is never see my daughter again."

Rage welled up inside Reeve. "You can't buy me, now or ever. I love Clea and I *will* see her again. I'll get her back!"

Moore's face reddened momentarily then regained its natural color. "You haven't even heard my price, Holden," he said calmly, naming a very substantial sum, more money, indeed, than Reeve ever expected to earn.

"All the money in the world isn't enough. I will see her again," Reeve repeated.

This time Moore didn't contain his rage. He stood up, shaking a tight fist at Reeve with the warning, "No, you won't, Holden. That much I guarantee. You've had your chance, a good one, and you blew it, which was a mistake considering that the outcome remains the same."

He closed the checkbook and returned it to his vest pocket. "It's time for me to play hardball now."

The full extent of Moore's power became clear almost immediately. Reeve was assigned to battleship duty, and less than a week after his orders were out, he was aboard a military flight bound for Japan.

He tried to reach Clea through an address in Switzerland Charlie came up with, but all of his letters were returned unopened. Eventually, after months of waiting and hoping, Reeve came to realize that it was useless to fight the Moores and the hold they had on their daughter. Clea had made her choice, and she had not chosen him.

And he had his own life to live. When he got out of the Navy, he began to live it, on his own terms, and managed to forget about her, most of the time.

Until today. She'd walked back into his life, and he'd made the mistake of grabbing her and kissing her. Damn, it had been the wrong thing to do, but his emotions were so near the surface that holding them back became impossible.

He poured out the coffee and replaced it with Scotch. Then he poured that out. He had a lot of thinking to do, about Clea and himself and about Charlie. Clea's visit had brought back many memories, both good and bad, and he needed time—and a clear head—to sort them out.

CLEA WAS LOSING HER COOL. She usually projected an aura of calm and control when she worked, but her composure was slipping away, and it wasn't the first time.

"No, my dear, not that angle; it just won't work," whined Eric Lambert, who'd decorated the home Clea was photographing for *Trends* magazine.

She heard the words and tried to ignore them, but the frustration grew as she continued shooting. It had all begun the day before she saw Reeve, as if some sort of premonition had been at work, telling her to beware.

On the last shoot it had been the model's dress and the makeup man's love life that got to her; today it was the decorator's ego, a familiar problem she usually worked around. Usually.

"Clea, please." The voice was more insistent, causing Clea to lower her camera and look across at the speaker. "My lowboy isn't getting properly featured from that angle," he explained.

Clea knew all she had to do was take a couple of shots from the other side and smile sweetly. They wouldn't be used in the layout, but Eric would be happy. Somehow, she didn't care whether Eric was happy or not, just as she hadn't cared about the model or the makeup man.

"No, Eric," she said as she changed lenses, "the lowboy looks fine, and besides it's not the focus of the room. I know what the magazine wants."

"But, Clea . . ."

Clea clicked the lens in place, went on shooting and let Eric fume.

Hours later, she pulled the last print from the chemical bath, clipped it on the line with the others to dry and pulled off her rubber gloves. The amber safelight in her darkroom gave a comforting glow that had always made Clea feel somehow protected, knowing this was where she belonged. Tonight the familiar feeling of security wasn't there.

She was thinking about Reeve's boat. He'd always said he would have one someday. A pipe dream, according to her dad, but Reeve had made the dream happen.

Photojournalism had been her dream, and she'd pursued it for a while as a staff photographer for the *Times.* Then she'd moved on to something much safer, easier, and certainly better paying. She thought about the loss of that dream, and the one she and Reeve had shared, to sail the world. With her camera on that trip, she might have begun something very different. But of course that never happened, just as her life with Reeve never happened.

"There'll be other young men," her mother promised. But there never had been, not anyone like Reeve.

And now she'd found him again. Clea should have known Reeve wouldn't help with Charlie's predicament. She didn't know why she bothered to ask, unless she just wanted to see him again after all those years. That was part of it—finding him the same, learning that he wasn't married, admitting, to herself at least, that the attraction was still there.

She couldn't shake the memory of his kiss. There had been anger in it and passion, too, and it made her vividly aware of what remained unfinished between them. She shouldn't have run from Reeve.

Clea pushed the thoughts out of her head. Standing in the middle of the darkroom, daydreaming about what might have been, certainly wasn't going to help Charlie. He was the one who should be utmost in her mind, Clea told herself. She took off her apron, hung it on the door and went into the studio. There was still equipment to be unpacked. After that, she had some phone calls to make. She'd take Reeve's advice—fly down to Santa Inez and find Charlie on her own.

REEVE TURNED OFF THE ENGINE and sat in his Jeep in front of Clea's studio. The door was ajar, and he could see light through the window, but he didn't get out. Finding Clea's address had been easy enough; what wasn't easy was the answer to one pervasive question: why the hell was he here?

He hadn't meant to get involved, but the pull of the past was too hard to untangle. Maybe this would do it—getting Charlie out of one last jam, then cutting the ties with the Moore family once and for all.

He approached the studio quietly. Clea was unloading a huge canvas bag that held a variety of lights and stands, which she carefully stored in the corner as he watched.

She was dressed for hard work in jeans and an old shirt that completely covered her hips. A far-from-provocative outfit, it nevertheless made Reeve ache with remembrance as he watched her move around the room. He knew exactly how she looked and felt under the baggy shirt. He could almost see the glow of her naked skin, feel its soft curves, taste its saltiness and sweetness.

He could have stood and watched all night, his senses alive and filled with her, but he finally tapped at the door to get her attention.

Her lips parted, but she remained silent for a moment. "Come in," she said finally. "I'm just unloading."

"Let me help you."

"No, it's all right. I'm almost finished." She unloaded the last light stands and put the bag away while

Reeve watched, feeling helpless here in her domain. He almost wished they were on the boat where he could be in charge.

When Clea finished, she stood in the middle of the room, looking at him, waiting. The moment was awkward, reverberating with their meeting aboard the *Argosy*.

"I like your studio," he said, forcing himself to make conversation. It was a big room, one side lined in no-seam paper for portrait shots, the rest crammed with equipment and books relating to photography, the walls filled with glossy photos, not all of them in color. He moved around the studio, looking at the black-and-white shots, portraits of ordinary people in ordinary circumstances, old men, working women, children. In one photograph a young boy was facing down a competitor in the schoolyard; in another two little girls were jumping rope.

"I like these very much," he said. "They're powerful." He avoided mentioning the glossy colored shots, which had made their way to covers of chic national magazines.

"I took them during what I suppose you'd call a more serious phase."

He moved close to where she stood and looked down at her. "We all change, Clea. Even I've changed."

Because she had no idea what that was leading to, Clea didn't respond.

"I'm going to Mexico."

She felt her heart lift. "Oh, thank you, Reeve," she said with relief.

"It seems, well, right for me to bail him out once more. I couldn't help thinking about the old times, the good times."

"Oh, Reeve, I'm so glad."

"I wrestled with this a long time yesterday. I thought of what you said about loyalty. Hell, Charlie might have been a pain in the neck with the midnight calls to pick him up in Vegas or Tahoe." He couldn't resist a smile. "Did he ever tell you about the two Darlenes?"

Clea shook her head.

"Somehow your brother got engaged to two women named Darlene at the same time. Neither knew about the other, and Charlie swore he hadn't actually asked them to marry him, so he concocted this scheme to get out of both engagements."

"I'm afraid to ask," Clea said.

Reeve laughed. "It was pretty crazy. Charlie wanted me to pretend I was his psychiatrist and tell the Darlenes he was mentally incompetent. With Charlie a lie was always the easiest solution, although in this case he wasn't far off about his mental state."

Reeve let his voice trail off before picking up the story again. "However, as usual, I avoided the lie and told them the truth. It required a lot of hand-holding on my part, and both the women continued to contact me for months. Even when they knew the truth, they wanted him back."

"It's hard to stay angry at him, isn't it?"

Reeve didn't answer directly. "He came through when I needed him. He loaned me the money for the *Argosy.*"

"I didn't know. He's always been generous."

"Yeah, a prince of a guy," Reeve replied, reverting to his old cynicism. "We'll canonize him later. Meanwhile I'll take the *Argosy* to Mexico to see what kind of trouble he's in. Charlie's my oldest friend. It's the least I can do."

"I'm very grateful."

Reeve held up a cautionary hand. "Don't be grateful yet. I haven't left. I don't have a crew, and I might not be able to find Charlie when I get there."

Only one phrase hung in Clea's mind. "No crew?"

"I promised my mate some time off. His wife's due to have a baby anytime now."

"Surely you can pick up someone else," she said, anxiety replacing her earlier excitement.

He shrugged. "It could take a day or two, even a week."

"I'm not sure we can wait," she said, almost panicky at the idea that Reeve might back out. Charlie needed him, and she was determined the trip wasn't going to fall through. Her mind worked frantically and before she thought, the words were out. "I can crew for you."

Reeve opened his mouth to answer, but Clea didn't give him a chance. "I'd be flying to Santa Inez anyway. Why not sail with you? We could leave at once. To-morrow...anytime."

"It's not a good idea," he said flatly.

"You mean because of yesterday..."

Reeve ran his fingers through his hair. "I'm sorry about that, Clea."

"It was difficult for both of us, seeing each other after so many years. I guess we were both a little crazy." She tried to lighten her words by adding a smile.

Reeve let out a deep breath. So that was how she was handling it, making the kiss a part of their past, excusing it because of what had gone on before. He would play along with that, but it still didn't mean he was going to agree to the rest. He wasn't going to take her on the trip.

"Yesterday aside, I don't think it's a good idea for you to sail to Mexico with me."

"I think it's a great idea. In fact, the more I think about it, the better it seems. You need a crew; I want to get to Charlie. If you're worried about us, don't, Reeve. We saw each other again, and we survived. Now we can move on. Here we are now, talking about Charlie, making plans—well, *I'm* making plans," she added with a laugh. "I think we can do it; I think we can be friends now."

"Friends," Reeve repeated thoughtfully. "That seems strange after all this time."

"But not impossible?"

"Maybe not," he admitted.

"Two friends on a quest. I like the sound of that. It could be a challenge to find Charlie, and ourselves, as well."

Reeve could feel himself weakening, but he gave his argument one more shot. "It might be a rough sail."

"I'm a pretty good sailor. Remember when we used to take Daddy's little speedboat out, you and me and Charlie and his girl of the moment?"

"You'd insist on standing on the bow looking for whales no matter how we yelled at you." He'd forgotten, and now it came back to him—Clea, tanned and lithe, the sea spraying her face, her blond hair a cloud around her head. The memory made him ache.

"I never fell overboard," she boasted.

"That's hardly a qualification."

"Come on, Reeve, you know I can do it."

"I haven't said yes."

"But there's no reason not to unless you can't handle our friendship or just don't want me around. Which is it?"

He answered her question with one of his own. "What about all this?" His gesture took in the studio. "You can't just walk away from it."

"Yes I can," she said. "I'll reschedule what I can and give everything else to other photographers. We're a club, you know. There's always someone who can cover for me."

"And do as good a job?" he asked.

Clea smiled slyly. "Maybe not, but if they want me badly enough, they'll have to wait. So what's your answer, Captain?"

His response was hesitant. "I guess it seems sensible. There's no reason we can't be friends, and if you're going to this place in Mexico anyway—"

"Santa Inez," she provided.

"Then we'll sail together. I need to warn you that I run a tight ship."

"Aye, aye, Captain," she teased, throwing him a salute.

It was all business now. "See you Friday then, around five-thirty, and that's a.m. I plan to be under sail by six."

"I won't be late," she promised.

CLEA LOCKED UP THE STUDIO and climbed the stairs to her apartment. Well, the rules were set; they'd agreed—two friends out to help Charlie, the past behind them.

But they didn't have to forget the past; they could accept it. That was healthier. After long hours of hauling ropes and scrubbing the deck and falling into bed exhausted, she'd lose the butterflies that beat wildly in her abdomen when she looked at him. They'd talk, and in talking the past would no longer be their enemy. When they parted it would be as friends. Then she could get on with her life. Clea stopped to look out at the ocean and wondered who the hell she was trying to fool.

She changed her mind a thousand times in the next two days. Once she became so firmly committed to her decision *not* to go that she actually decided to call him.

Her speech was all prepared: it was a terrible idea for them to travel all that distance together, and it wouldn't help Charlie at all. She would stick to her original plan and fly down, meeting Reeve in Santa Inez. Reeve could take it from there, and if she could be of help, she'd be nearby. That was the new plan, or the old plan rethought.

But he didn't have a listed number, and Clea remembered she hadn't seen a phone aboard the *Argosy*.

So she called her parents to tell them she'd be out of town for a while and found herself drawn into a long conversation. It ended with her accepting a dinner invitation she'd just as soon have ignored, knowing she'd have to tell them about Charlie. But Clea was determined to keep Reeve out of it. She knew what the mere mention of his name would do to her parents, especially her father.

At the end of the dinner, Clea's mother smiled fondly at her daughter. "This doesn't happen often—a quiet family evening."

"Hardly the whole family without Charlie," Charles Moore said pointedly. Ten years had added a few pounds to his frame, silver to his hair, but he was still a formidable presence. "Jeanine tells me he's in Mexico."

Clea didn't need to be intentionally vague about Charlie's circumstances; she really knew very little. "He's in a town called Santa Inez. I thought it might be fun to go down and join him."

"Is he there on business or pleasure?" Moore quizzed.

"I'm not sure," Clea answered. "Probably business."

As Moore raised his eyebrows doubtfully, his wife chimed in. "Charlie has such talent. There really isn't anything he can't do if he sets his mind to it."

"Mother's right. Charlie always had great ideas," Clea agreed.

"Your defense of your brother is nothing new," Moore chided.

"I can't help it," Clea defended. She couldn't. Her father was right, and so was Reeve.

"Charlie is . . . well, special." Jeanine's brown eyes, that were just a shade lighter than her daughter's, softened. "I only wish he'd settle down. Of course, I wish that for both of my children." A pensive look invaded her face. "I saw Richard last week."

Clea didn't even blink at the mention of her ex-fiancé. "How is he?"

"He looks wonderful, and he's very successful, I hear. His law practice is growing by leaps and bounds."

"He's a great guy," Clea said, "and I'm happy for him, but I really don't care about Richard, Mother." She'd said that often before, but it always seemed necessary during her mother's confrontations. This time she softened her words with an excuse. "I've been too involved in my work for romance."

"So involved you can run off to Mexico, eh?" Charles had never been able to resist baiting his children.

"Exactly. After all that hard work, it's time for a rest," Clea replied.

"Well, not a long one, I hope," Jeanine said. "Peggy Rothberg called me yesterday, and I think I have a nice little job for you."

Clea groaned inwardly. She never had the heart to turn down the "nice little jobs" that came her way through the Moores' friends. They were lucrative, she had to admit, but Clea was finding them less and less interesting, wondering how many designer-decorated homes she could photograph without getting stale— how many coming-out parties and wedding anniversaries . . . How long had it been since she'd tried anything different? She drew her mind back to what her mother was saying.

"Judson Rothberg is celebrating his sixty-fifth next month, and of course Peggy wants you to shoot the party."

"I'll call her when I get back, but I may not take the job." Clea ignored the hurt look on her mother's face. Jeanine Moore was a master at manipulation—a formidable weapon she'd often used against her children.

Jeanine sighed deeply, painfully. "I told Peggy I was sure she could count on you. She's such a good friend— how embarrassing . . ." The words trailed sadly away. Jeanine controlled by silence and doleful looks as skillfully as her husband ruled by force of personality.

This time Clea refused to take the bait. Instead, she answered evenly, "I feel as though I'm getting in a rut— taking easy work, like the Rothbergs, to avoid more serious challenges."

"But, dear, no one will pay you for photos of dirty little children and run-down docks. As for photojournalism, well, I'm just glad you aren't working for the newspaper anymore," Jeanine said.

Clea managed a laugh. "It was good experience, but I could certainly never make a living on staff at the newspaper. Photographic essays are different, though.

I can do them on my own, and it's time for some diversity."

"Burnout," her father announced. "We all get it. Maybe this trip to Mexico is just what you need to get the juices stirred up again, get the blood racing and the fires burning."

Clea turned away and looked out across the smooth green lawn. Her father might be closer to the truth than he realized.

3

THEY SET SAIL two days later with a brisk following wind. After a few hours the wind shifted, and Reeve began a long series of tacks, first to starboard, then to port.

"Ready to come about," Reeve called from his place at the helm.

Clea answered with a casual wave of her hand, almost like a seasoned sailor, she thought, feeling pretty good that she was not only pulling her weight but that she and Reeve were a team. Working the sails was becoming almost automatic. Just when her confidence began to soar, it happened. The *Argosy* refused to come about, the sails began to luff wildly into the wind, and the boat started drifting backward.

"Grab the jib sheet, haul it in, Clea." Reeve's voice called across the sound of flapping sails.

"I am—I mean, I'm trying," she yelled back. The sail pulled frantically, like a living thing determined to be free now that the wind had it. Clea jerked at the sheet, which was slipping through her hands, winding a loop around her palm. She held on even though the abrasive hemp was cutting into her skin.

As the boat wallowed in long troughs, Clea had a momentary vision of a sudden rough wave, an unexpected burst of wind, tossing her overboard. Automatically, her muscles tensed. "And I chose not to fly to Santa Inez!" she muttered as she bent her knees and braced her feet on the damp, slippery deck, trying to gain leverage. Her shoulder muscles strained, her arms quivered as she fought the wind and jib sheet until slowly, almost imperceptibly she felt herself winning. Bit by bit, the sail began to respond.

Then Reeve was beside her, shouldering her out of the way as he reached for the line. "Let me do that. You grab the tiller," he ordered gruffly. "Put it starboard."

Clea's resentment flared as she backed away and took the tiller, holding it steady until they were on course again and tacking into the wind. She kept her determination to abide by orders until Reeve came back to the helm, then she lost her cool. "Dammit, Reeve, I could have handled the jib," she said. "There was no need to wrestle me out of the way."

"I didn't wrestle you, and I couldn't wait all day, Clea," he replied, his eyes busy checking the sails.

The criticism stung Clea, who was more than ready to fight back. "It might have been your fault for jamming the tiller—"

"I don't care whose fault it was. The point is that it needed to be handled fast." He looked at the sails again. "Now we need a favoring wind and don't have one. I think I'll stow the sails and go ahead under power."

"Not on my account," Clea said, her eyes flashing. "I can handle the sailing without any special considerations."

"It has nothing to do with you," came the response. "I told you before you signed on that I'm the captain and I make the decisions."

"Aye, aye, sir," Clea said, and this time there was no humor in her voice.

As it turned out, the work didn't end with striking the sails. There was always something to do, some assign-

ment that Reeve gave her in a cool, impersonal way.
Clea did whatever he asked, all the while cursing under her breath the decision not to fly to Santa Inez.

She managed to grab a few hours of sleep, and just
before sunrise Reeve awakened her with the happy news
of a favoring wind. They'd take the day ahead under
sail and make it to San Diego. Clea gritted her teeth and
rolled out of the bunk.

Twelve hours later she collapsed in the small forward cabin that Reeve had assigned her, hands blis-
tered from the sheets, back and shoulders aching from
the pull and weight of the sails. She couldn't remember
sitting down all day. Even when Reeve had asked her
to take the wheel, she'd stood, too nervous to relax.

It wasn't yet sunset, but they'd anchored just south
of San Diego for the night, to Clea's relief. She didn't
think she could have gone another minute, and she had
a feeling Reeve knew that. If he'd had a second mate
along, a man, with more experience, they could have
sailed on into the evening.

Well, she might not be a man, might not have the experience necessary for Reeve's requirements, but she'd
shown him she could take anything he dished out.
There'd been no mistakes and no arguments, just his
orders and her compliance, like captain and crew.

Now all she wanted was a few minutes' rest.

Just as she closed her eyes, there was a knock on the
door. She answered it with a moan.

Reeve opened the hatch and stood looking down at
her. He was wearing his bathing suit and had wrapped
a towel around his neck.

Clea returned his gaze, her eyes taking in his lean,
tanned body. Quickly, she looked away, but it was too
late. The image prevailed. Reeve's powerful chest,

muscular arms and legs, his body so like an athlete's, had enraptured her as a teenager and did exactly that now. There was no denying the attraction, but she denied it just the same, willing herself to look at him with her face remaining unreadable.

"Am I working you too hard?" he asked.

Clea swung her long legs to the floor. "Of course not. I feel great." Then at the look of disbelief on his face, she laughed. "I'm lying. These have been about the hardest two days of my life, but a good night's sleep will do wonders. I'll be ready for the last leg of the sail." She spoke with more verve than she felt.

"You plan to turn in now?" he asked, and Clea could see disappointment on his face.

"Yes," she answered.

"It's only six o'clock."

"Time means nothing to aching bones," she countered.

"I know a better solution than sleep."

"Oh?"

"A swim. It'll help you unwind. It'll help me, too, I'll admit. We've both been on edge."

"Sorry about yesterday and the jib sheet . . ." she began.

"Just normal shakedown with a new crew. It's always tough, and you're doing great," he complimented. "I'm a bear the first day or two. Now, come on, let's work out some kinks with a swim. See you on deck in five minutes." With that he ducked through the hatch, leaving Clea sitting mutely on the bunk.

Finally she got up and groped in her duffel for a bathing suit, determined to keep up with Reeve. The invitation to a swim was his first overture of friendship after all the orders he'd given her. No matter how tired, she was going to meet him halfway.

Reeve was already in the water when she came on deck. He shouted at her. "Come on in. I've done a shark survey, and they're all dining elsewhere."

The joke didn't faze Clea, who'd swum off Southern California beaches all of her life. She dove in, absorbing the initial shock then realizing that the water here was warmer than the frigid surf of Venice.

She came up right beside him and quickly wished her dive had been less perfectly positioned. They were almost touching. Perhaps Reeve didn't feel the electric tension between them, but Clea felt it, and it was unsettling. Quickly, she swam a few strokes away.

She turned to see the boat lit by the red glow of the setting sun and called out to him. "I see why the *Argosy* is the love of your life. She's beautiful."

Reeve swam toward her, his strong arms cutting the water cleanly with a stroke she remembered so well.

"The *Argosy*'s very special," he said, "and worth it most of the time." He didn't explain the remark but smiled at Clea, his teeth amazingly white against his tanned skin, his dark hair glistening. He was so close that if Clea took a half stroke her body would bump against his. She quickly put more space between them.

"So you want to race, do you?" he called out.

"Not tonight," she said, turning and treading water.

"I thought you were a regular water baby," he teased, closing the space again. "Remember the first time I saw you?"

She didn't have to answer. He knew she remembered.

"You'd just finished laps in the pool, and I would have sworn you were an Olympic contender. You could have been, Clea," he said more seriously.

"Maybe," she half agreed. "But not now. I haven't even been in the water in months. I'm really out of shape."

"Not you," Reeve said. "At least, not from what I've seen."

Clea felt herself blush with pleasure that Reeve liked what he saw after so many years. It was silly, Clea knew, but all of a sudden she felt wonderful. Maybe, she decided, it was time for that race.

She found a surge of energy and dove beneath the surface. When she appeared a few yards away, she called out, "Reeve, I was lying again. I do want to race." Not waiting for his answer, she took off for the boat.

She was swimming hard, but he was right behind her. Confident he couldn't catch up, Clea relaxed a little. She hadn't counted on his playfulness. The contest had become a game, and when he got close enough, he lunged forward and caught her foot. Clea tried to kick him loose, but he held fast, one hand closing on her ankle and pulling her toward him.

She kicked futilely then gave up as she felt herself sliding along the length of his body. His hands moved forward, capturing her calves, then her thighs. She struggled again, but one arm was around her waist. It was over; he was beside her, laughing. "No fair cheating the captain, Clea."

Their faces were inches apart. He gave his head a shake, and water cascaded down his cheeks and across his forehead. There was a light in his eyes that she hadn't seen since the old days, a look of conspiracy and joy.

Instinctively, Clea reached out and held onto his shoulders as she'd done so often in the past. She remembered the feeling of his muscles hard and tight beneath her hands, and just as he'd always done, Reeve grabbed her around the waist as they bobbed in the water. The rays of sun bathed him in a rosy glow, and Clea almost laughed aloud at the happiness she felt. It was as if they were kids again; it was wonderful.

"Is it your nature to cheat? Shame on you," he teased, still caught up in the moment.

"I didn't cheat. I only took advantage of the situation." She tilted her chin back, challenging.

"I'll remember that when *I* have the advantage." Reeve smiled at her, his eyes unreadable. He was still smiling when he turned away, then turned back again, and without any advance notice, dunked her.

Clea came up sputtering, thrashing out to grab him, but he was at the ladder, pulling himself onto the deck. "Last one dressed has to do the dishes," he called out.

Quickly, Clea headed for the boat and climbed aboard. The swim had turned out better than she imagined. For the first time, things between them were easy and natural.

The mood remained light during dinner, which Reeve laid out on a table at the stern. Clea was both pleased and surprised. The night before, they'd each taken cold cuts to their cabins. Tonight the food was the same, sliced chicken and roast beef, but the ambience was very different.

"I remembered we had rolls for sandwiches. Forgot them last night," he apologized. "And there's fruit again, but," he added with a flourish, pulling out a bottle, "I found some wine."

"That's a lovely touch," Clea said, joining him at the table.

"Oh, I've learned some refinements along the way."

She wasn't sure whether there'd been an edge of sarcasm in the comment or not, but she chose to think not. "I feel very pampered."

"Don't forget," he reminded her, "that you do the dishes."

As they shared the meal they talked casually about the boats they'd seen that morning, the school of porpoises that followed them for a while, and the brief squall they'd run through shortly after leaving the harbor the day before. It was an easy conversation, none of it intimate— a nice change, Clea thought, from the near silence of the day before.

She finished the last bite of her sandwich and leaned back in the chair. "Good food, fine wine, great company, and sunset over the Pacific. How could anyone ask for more?" To her it was an offhand remark, but Reeve's response was more intense.

"It's all I've ever wanted." When Clea looked at him, his face was unreadable. Then he smiled. "All I really need is the ocean. Your company is a plus since charters don't always make good companions."

"It's paradise," Clea said. "A million miles separate me and the darkroom."

"You'll miss it in a few days," he predicted.

She wasn't going to disagree. It was much more pleasant when they weren't arguing. "Maybe," she said, "and maybe not. Right now I much prefer being on the ocean to looking out at it as I climb the stairs to my apartment. I never seem to have time to relax."

"Obviously, you work too hard."

"I do," she admitted. "Sometimes I wonder why." Then she laughed softly. "I know why. There's nothing else in my life."

He looked away from her across the waves, his eyes hidden. "What about the guy you almost married?" he asked finally.

"I wasn't in love with him," she answered honestly, "and I'd never marry a man I didn't love."

It was very quiet then with only the lapping of the waves against the hull. Clea could hear her own breath and his. The moment seemed suspended. Was he remembering what they'd once sworn to each other?

I'll never love another man, Reeve.

I'll love you forever, until the day I die, Clea.

Reeve broke the silence. "I guess there're all different kinds of love. We learn that as we get older."

They were talking about love and marriage now, and Clea realized that she wanted to know about his ex-wife, but it seemed as though he wasn't going to help her. She took a deep breath. "Your marriage . . ." Her voice trailed off.

He understood and was willing to answer. "Susan was a great pal. I met her after the Navy, before I bought the *Argosy*. I was living in Seattle, and I tried to make it as a landlubber because that's what she wanted—a guy who'd come home at five every night to a white picket fence and a house filled with kids."

"And what did *you* want?" It seemed very important to hear his answer.

"I wanted children eventually, but I wasn't ready then, and I wasn't ready for the rest of it ever. I wanted to be at sea, traveling. I wanted this." He waved his hand over the horizon. "Our marriage wasn't fair to her or to me. I hear from her occasionally. She's remarried and has a baby. My getting out of her life was the best thing that could have happened to us." He smiled ruefully. "I'm becoming philosophical in my old age. Who would have thought it?"

"Life has a funny way of working out," Clea said. "All of yesterday and most of today I was wishing I hadn't insisted on sailing with you, especially when we had that round over the sail when you were so distant and official with me."

"Just shy," he said with a burst of honesty, "and on edge about us being together. I was afraid we'd be at swords' points the whole time."

So he'd been nervous, too. Somehow that made Clea more comfortable with her own anxiety. "It was probably good that we yelled at each other early on and got it all out."

Reeve looked at her and smiled. "When I saw you lying on the bunk in your cabin, I thought you might demand that I take you home."

"No such luck. I'm in this for the duration. Until we get to Santa Inez and find Charlie."

The mention of her brother's name changed Reeve's tone. "Oh, yes. Charlie. Well, the old boy never stays put very long, does he? Tomorrow we should know what's going on."

"Tomorrow." She repeated the word. "It seems so soon."

Reeve looked as though he were going to agree. Then he said quickly, "We can't do anything to change that." His expression was guarded. Clea didn't try to read anything in it.

Reeve got to his feet. "Tomorrow *morning* will certainly come soon. I need to check the lines and set the lights. I'm not usually so derelict in my duties."

Clea stood up, too, and began stacking the dishes as he passed them to her. Even though she didn't look up, she could feel his eyes following her as she carried the plates into the galley. When she came back he was standing at the door, blocking her way. They were so close that she could hear him breathing, deep and easy. She was able to avoid his eyes and concentrate on the rise and fall of his chest. He was waiting, but she didn't know what he was waiting for.

Neither of them moved. Reeve was in the shadows, and the chiseled lines of his face were softened; the blue of his eyes was muted. It was the first time she'd seen that kind of gentleness on his face, and she was reminded of the old Reeve.

Reeve saw her look, and tried to interpret it. There was gratitude, he knew, but was there more? Her eyes were luminous in the soft light of the moon, her hair like spun gold. He could smell the light fragrance of her perfume and hear the gentle rhythm of her breathing.

Swimming beside her earlier had made Reeve realize that he was very close to the edge of his desire. He wanted to reach for her, hold her near. He knew exactly how her body would mold to his, how her head would fit against his shoulder. He could almost taste the sweetness of her lips.

He reached out, his hand about to touch her hair. Then he paused, unable to act on his desire and jeopardize what they'd salvaged tonight, those first tentative stirrings of friendship. Once his lips touched hers, he'd be lost, caught up in the passion that had never left him. He dropped his hand and spoke quietly, quickly.

"I'll give you a wake-up call in the morning. We'll need an early start." The words were dismissive, but this was one moment he didn't dare prolong.

"Good night, Reeve." Her voice was no more than a whisper, and she looked at him for an instant before turning away to her cabin. He wasn't sure what he saw in her face—relief, or disappointment.

"Good night, Clea," he called after her. "Sleep well." Then he, too, turned away.

4

THEY DOCKED AT DUSK after another long and hard day of sailing, but instead of feeling tired, Clea felt her nerves singing; she was strangely energized. She glanced at Reeve as he moored the boat, dropping a last line to secure them. He moved quickly and expertly but with a kind of anticipatory energy that mirrored her own. She'd felt it all day, that excitement they shared.

For a moment it seemed familiar, like the times long ago when they were together on their own kind of adventure. He looped the line into a perfect holding knot and looked at her. The setting sun caught in his hair, creating an exciting aureole all around him. Against the backlight, Clea couldn't see Reeve's expression, but she sensed a glint that could have been mistaken for so many things.

Shaking away the possibilities, Clea decided it was nothing more than her feeling of relief that they were in Santa Inez at last, closing in on Charlie. With any luck they'd find him within the hour.

AS SHE WAITED BESIDE REEVE for the customs officer to scan her passport, her gaze swept up toward the town. She saw its picture-postcard quaintness, but she wondered if there were something pulsating below the surface beauty to give the town an edge. While as a photojournalist she hoped for something more; as

Charlie's sister she hoped everything was just as it seemed—that her brother was safe here.

"What do you think?" Reeve asked.

"It's certainly pretty," Clea answered. "Not a likely place for Charlie to get in trouble."

"Your brother can get in trouble in paradise," Reeve answered as he pocketed his passport.

"Just like Adam?" Clea responded.

"He had Eve to blame," Reeve fired back, and Clea saw a spark of humor in his eyes.

The customs officer returned her passport with barely a glance. He was used to tourists, and his sleepy-eyed gaze told Clea that he knew what these two Americans were there for—a weekend of sun, lobster, tequila and romance. He was just about to wave them on when Clea asked him a question in her most careful Spanish.

"*Por favor, señor, donde esta La Paloma Blanca?*" The White Dove Resort had been Charlie's last address in Santa Inez.

The officer smiled at her attempt to speak his language and broke into a tirade or rapid Spanish in response, accompanied by much waving of the hands and pointing.

Clea listened, smiled and with profuse thanks took Reeve's arm and steered him toward the plaza.

"That sounded complicated enough to be directions to Mexico City," he commented.

"My ability to translate is definitely rusty," she admitted, "but I got the general idea."

"Glad to hear it. I didn't get past the first sentence," Reeve said as they crossed the plaza to a line of waiting taxis. "Do we grab one or shall we walk?"

"Taxi," Clea suggested without a moment's hesitation, unwilling to trust her rendition of the directions.

They took the first cab in the line, an American car of uncertain vintage, and were whisked away, leaving a puff of black smoke behind as they negotiated the narrow streets toward the hotel.

"Ah, La Paloma Blanca," the driver exclaimed. "Many Americans stay there. Very beautiful. Very expensive."

"Only the best for brother Charlie," Reeve muttered, eliciting no response from Clea. The sarcasm wasn't necessary, but on the other hand she couldn't disagree with his assessment.

"We probably should have changed clothes," Clea decided, uncomfortable in her shorts and Topsiders. She'd put on an oversize shirt to cover her skimpy T-shirt, tied the shirttails at the waist and pulled her windblown hair back in a loose braid, but the result was definitely casual. "This isn't quite the called-for dress at an elegant resort."

"Expensive doesn't always mean elegant," Reeve replied. "Besides, these resorts are used to casual dress."

"Not at dinnertime," Clea responded, reminding him unintentionally that she'd traveled among the world's jet-setters most of her life and knew what was de rigueur. He didn't respond, to her relief. In fact, when she gave him a sideways glance, he seemed perfectly relaxed beside her, comfortable in his shorts and T-shirt, legs and arms bronzed, eyes hidden behind dark glasses.

The warmth from the night before that had lingered over into the morning seemed to have faded as they left the boat. That was for the best, Clea argued to herself.

They'd find Charlie soon, then the quest would be over. No harm done to either of them.

And yet the time had passed so quickly. There was so much she'd wanted to say to Reeve, should have said on the boat. Now it was probably too late. Instead of being glad that she was in Santa Inez, Clea was wishing they'd had more time.

The taxi pulled up at the hotel's portico. Low pastel-colored buildings, roofed in the inevitable red tile, were covered with a profusion of flowers and surrounded by palm trees interspersed with random fountains and meandering streams. More picture-postcard beauty, Clea thought as she heard the sounds of children splashing and shouting in the pool.

"Shall I wait for you, *señor?*" the driver asked.

Reeve looked at Clea then nodded. "Good idea. You never know; we may need you again."

Hoping he was wrong, Clea walked beside Reeve along tiled paths, past more fountains into the ornate hotel lobby.

Before they reached the desk, Reeve stopped and looked at Clea. "Okay," he said, "what's the game plan?"

Clea looked around then answered, "I suppose we should talk with the desk clerk and see if Charlie's still registered. If so, all we have to do is give him a call." She knew that was too easy; Charlie hadn't asked for help because he was enjoying himself at a resort hotel.

"And if not?" Reeve asked simply.

"If not, well, then . . . I don't know," Clea stumbled. "Interview other employees?" Her uncertainty came through, and at Reeve's grin she added, "This sleuthing is new to me."

"I'm an amateur myself," he said, "but I suppose we can ask a few questions without arousing suspicions. You check out the desk clerk since your Spanish is good."

She had to laugh at that.

"Well, much better than mine," he added. "I'll wander into the bar and talk to a few tourists. I guarantee Charlie spent some time there. Why don't we meet out on the patio?"

Clea nodded and all but slinked away, feeling very much like a B-movie character.

Fifteen minutes later, totally deflated, she joined Reeve at his table on the patio.

"No luck, eh?" he asked. He was sipping a frosty Mexican beer and had ordered a glass of wine for Clea.

"No luck, but something's going on. I had to really prod the desk clerk to get him to pull the records. He finally admitted that Charlie had been here, which I knew already, and added that he'd checked out and left no address, which I suspected. Then the desk clerk walked away."

Clea took a sip of wine. "I mean he just disappeared, Reeve. No explanation, no nothing. When he finally came back he looked at me as if he couldn't imagine what I was waiting for and said he had nothing else to tell me. I asked to see the manager." Clea let herself smile. "You can imagine the response I got to that request."

"The manager's off sick?" Reeve guessed.

"On vacation," Clea corrected. "I definitely got the runaround, which I don't like one bit." Clea took another sip of her wine. "What did you find out?"

"A little more," Reeve said. "Finish your wine and relax."

"Reeve, what is it?"

"Relax, I said. It's all right."

Clea couldn't comply. "Please, tell me what's happened. Is he—"

"He's alive," Reeve assured her quickly, "but apparently he's had an accident."

"An accident?" Clea could feel her heart pounding as her mind raced off in all directions, imagining every possible scenario.

"Well, not exactly. From what I can figure out, your brother was beaten up."

"A fight?" Clea felt almost relieved. Charlie certainly had been in enough of those.

"Maybe," Reeve said, "but it sounded more like a working over."

Clea was puzzled.

"Like some guys ganged up on him," Reeve explained.

Clea felt her heart constrict. She was used to Charlie's fights, but being beaten by a gang was another matter. Charlie could be very seriously hurt this time.

Clea was ready to leave, to go to Charlie immediately. "Where is he?" she asked.

Reeve took her arm and settled her back into the chair from which Clea had half risen. "Just sit down, Clea, and I'll tell you what I know. This happened several days ago so we don't need to go rushing after him."

Clea tried to relax as she finished her wine and Reeve told her the rest. "The bartender remembers that an ambulance was called. He believes they took Charlie to the closest hospital, less than a half hour away."

"Then why didn't the desk clerk tell me?" Anger was mixed with her concern for Charlie.

"To avoid bad PR, I would guess. Certainly they aren't going to admit a guest had the living daylights beaten out of him at Santa Inez's finest resort. That kind of thing might be acceptable on the waterfront, but not here. The answer is just to pretend none of it happened."

"But it did," Clea said, "and we should find the hospital and go there right away, Reeve."

"Clea, I told you another few minutes wasn't going to matter. Charlie is probably out of the hospital and on his way home. The least he could have done was call—"

"I'm sure if he'd been able to call he would have let us know he was all right. That's what worries me, Reeve. I have a feeling it's serious. Please—"

Clea's concern was written all over her face. Reeve couldn't have missed it or failed to respond to it. "All right." He stood up and dropped a few bills onto the table. "We'll go to the hospital, but I guarantee Charlie's okay. Your brother is too damned ornery to get badly hurt."

That made Clea smile again, and feeling better but still concerned she headed for the door with Reeve beside her, solicitous but totally calm.

"Glad you waited," Reeve said to the cabdriver as they got in. "We're going to the hospital."

"Which one?" came the question.

Reeve leaned back against the seat, shaking his head. "From what I understand, there's only one—outside of town."

"*Si,*" the driver agreed. "There is one outside of town to the north and another outside of town to the south."

"Do you want me to go ask the bartender?" Clea offered.

Reeve shook his head, addressing the driver again. "Which one is about two miles away?"

"To the north, *señor*."

"And the other, the one to the south?" Reeve asked.

"Oh, a long way—twenty, thirty miles," came the response, which caused Clea to laugh in spite of her concern.

"Head north then," Reeve said with only the hint of a smile.

"Good choice," came the driver's response as the cab pulled into traffic. "Fine facilities there, all the best."

From the outside, the hospital didn't seem to live up to the description. It was an old building that looked suspiciously like it had once been a museum, and inside the high ceilings and narrow halls opening into large anterooms did nothing to dispel the nonmedical image.

Clea and Reeve glanced at each other as they headed down a cavernous hall, but it was with some relief that they caught glimpses of modern equipment in the rooms they passed as doctors in crisp white coats went about their work with nuns in blue-and-white habits assisting.

Clea managed to make herself understood by one of the sisters who directed them to an information desk at the end of the hall. The mention of Charlie's name was enough. The young nun behind the desk lit up, a pretty smile on her face. "*El Señor Carlos?* He is in room 103. It is so good he has company. I am sure he has been very lonely."

As they headed for Charlie's room, Clea couldn't suppress a sense of relief. Although their footsteps echoed strangely through the baroque building, aspects of medical excellence were apparent. Whatever had happened to Charlie, he would be cared for here. But what had happened to him?

Clea hurried ahead and pushed open the door to room 103. There were four beds—three occupied, one by a very old man, the second by a teenager. A curtain was drawn around the third bed. Unhesitatingly, Clea stepped forward and pulled it back.

"Hi, Sis. Welcome to Santa Inez. What the hell took you so long?"

"Oh, Charlie." Clea felt her heart sink. Despite his irreverent words, Charlie had been very badly hurt. One arm was in a cast and one leg in traction. His head was bandaged, and bruises covered his face and chest.

"If you think I look bad now, you should have seen me a couple of days ago," he joked. "Unrecognizable. But the doctors tell me I'll be restored to my former handsome self, Sis, so not to worry."

Clea grabbed hold of the hand her brother offered. "I don't know whether to kiss you or strangle you," she said.

"Please, no more brutality," Charlie responded. "A kiss will do just fine."

Clea moved close, kissing him on the cheek and giving him a careful hug. In spite of her gentleness, she noticed that Charlie winced in pain.

He recovered quickly, holding out his hand to Reeve. "You old son of a gun," he said. "You finally came."

Reeve shrugged. "Some of us never learn." It was a remark that could have been taken as a joke, but Clea knew there was an element of seriousness in it.

"Pull up some chairs," Charlie said, "and make yourselves comfortable. It's more like a castle here than a hospital as you may have noticed. But the staff is damned competent."

"What do they say about your recovery?" Clea asked as she sat down, trying not to notice that Reeve remained standing.

"Coming along nicely is the phrase, and it's true. As soon as I get out of traction and get all the stitches removed—"

Clea winced, but her brother waved off her concern. "My scalp will look a little weird for a while, but no permanent damage done. The brain's still intact, such as it is," he added with a grin toward Reeve, who was prepared to get down to basics now that the health situation had been taken care of.

"Maybe you'll be able to offer us some facts then, since your brain is working. What exactly is going on?"

"Had an accident, old buddy."

"Obviously."

"We heard about the beating," Clea said, jumping in quickly, as anxious as Reeve to know the details now that she was assured Charlie would recover.

"Bad news travels fast, eh?" Seeing the serious looks on their faces, Charlie gave up his attempt at humor and asked, "Only the facts, ma'am?"

"Exactly," Reeve replied.

"Where shall I begin?" Charlie was hedging.

"At the beginning," Reeve suggested unsmilingly. "What were you doing in Santa Inez?"

"There was this deal," Charlie said, "one of the best of my life. I stumbled onto a great connection, a guy with a fabulous piece of art to sell—"

Reeve's eyebrows rose skeptically.

"I happened to know a buyer so I agreed to act as broker."

"Then why the SOS to me? That came before your accident." Reeve pressed.

"Yeah," Charlie acknowledged. "I tried to get in touch with you right away because I knew there was a possibility of running into problems. I needed someone I could trust. It was a touchy situation."

"I'll say." Reeve's glance swept over Charlie's battered form.

Clea was getting annoyed at the banter between the two men and insisted they get back to the story. "What went wrong?"

"Well, from what I can figure, my buyer changed his mind. He wanted the art, certainly, but he didn't want to pay the price. I had possession, and I expected a fair exchange, you know, money for merchandise. I guess I was a little naive."

Reeve remained silent, his eyes narrowing speculatively.

"You said you'd suspected something was wrong," she reminded her brother.

"True, but there's always that possibility, and when it came time to close the deal, I guess the thought of all that money went to my head. I forget to be careful. If Reeve had been with me . . ."

Reeve ignored the remark. "Your buyer sent goons down here to beat you up," he stated simply.

"That's about it." Charlie shifted a little in the bed. "And they did a fine job."

"I understand your problem, Charlie, and I'm sorry to see you in this situation, but I still don't see why Clea and I had to rush down here. Clearly you put out cash for the artwork. So you lost a bundle."

"Plus a small fortune when you consider what I was selling it for," Charlie added.

"So go to the police," Reeve suggested.

Charlie rolled his eyes to the ceiling. "You always were able to get to the heart of the matter, Reeve. But this time the simple solution is not an option. It turns out the artwork was stolen. I didn't know that, I swear," he added quickly just as the door swung open and a young doctor crossed to Charlie's bed, followed by a nun.

She spoke to them in clear and careful Spanish.

Clea translated for Reeve. "She wants us to leave for a few minutes so the doctor can examine Charlie."

"I got the gist of that," Reeve said with a half smile as they went into the hall.

Away from Charlie's hearing, Reeve was very blunt. "He's lying, Clea."

She wanted to deny that, but something told her Reeve was right.

"He'll have elaborate plans to retrieve this mysterious work of art, but don't expect me to comply. Charlie's loss is none of my business."

"I understand that, Reeve," Clea said. Clearly, Charlie had lost the money he paid for the artwork, but that money and the small fortune he stood to make on the deal were his problem, as Reeve said. They had found Charlie, and although he was injured, he would be all right. Nothing more could be expected of Reeve.

She smiled at him. "Thanks for helping me find my brother."

He touched her hand briefly. "It was a pleasant sailing trip."

The examination over, Clea and Reeve returned to Charlie's bedside but didn't return to the subject until the doctor and his nurse had left the room. Then Clea stepped in quickly.

"I think you need to tell us just what this mysterious piece of artwork is, Charlie. We want the whole story, not a revised version."

Charlie responded a little diffidently. "It's a jade carving—a jaguar."

"Come on Charlie," Reeve insisted. "Let's have it all."

"It's old—"

"How old?" Clea persisted.

"Pretty old." He saw Clea's face. "Very old. Olmec, actually."

"Olmec!" Clea was stunned. The Olmec civilization predated both the Mayan and Aztec in Mexico. Such carvings were rare; in fact they were hardly seen outside a museum. A terrible sinking feeling hit Clea suddenly. "This carving—was it stolen from a museum, Charlie?"

"Yes." Before she could respond, Charlie defended, "I didn't know, Sis, I really didn't. My fence didn't tell me where he got it. He swore it was from a reputable source."

"And what could be more reputable than a museum?" Reeve asked sarcastically before moving to the bed where he rested his hands on the iron frame and looked down at Charlie. "Now, old buddy, I don't know much about artifacts, Olmecs or Aztecs. I'm just an average kind of guy, but I know when a deal is too good to be true, and this is one of those deals."

Charlie said nothing, and Reeve pressed his advantage. "I see why you can't go to the police. If they get a whiff of your involvement, you're in deep trouble."

"I think they've already gotten a whiff."

Reeve frowned. "Have they questioned you?"

"No, but they're hanging around like they're just waiting for me to get out of here."

"There weren't any policemen in the hospital," Clea objected.

"They're outside," Charlie told his sister.

"How do you know?"

"I have ways," Charlie said. "Did you see them when you came in, Reeve?"

Reeve nodded, much to Clea's surprise. She'd seen nothing.

"That's why I need you, Reeve," Charlie said. There was perspiration forming on his forehead, whether from exhaustion or fear, Clea couldn't be sure.

"Oh, no, you don't," Reeve objected immediately.

Charlie wet his lips nervously. "I know where the jade is, but I can't prove it. I need your help, Reeve. Just hear me out. Carl Browning from Denver was my buyer. He has the jade; I'm sure of it. If we can somehow get it back or tell the museum exactly where it is, I'll get out of this without spending the rest of my life in a Mexican jail. But if the police can hang this on me—"

"And they probably can!" Clea snapped. She was torn between anger at Charlie's foolishness and fear that he would be found out and arrested. Despite his wheeling and dealing, he was family; he was her brother. And she was furious with him.

"So what's the bottom line here?" Reeve glanced at his watch to make a point. "You've been spinning a yarn for almost half an hour. Get on with it, Charlie."

Charlie took a deep breath. "I want you to find out exactly where Browning has the jade. That's all."

Reeve laughed but there was no amusement in the sound. "You actually want me to go to Colorado and find your artifact?"

"Reeve—"

"No way, Charlie. I'm not playing detective for you."

"I just want you to find out *if* Browning has the jade. That's all."

"Sorry, pal; you have the wrong guy, especially when you're still not telling us the truth."

Clea waited for an explanation, wondering what Reeve meant.

"Admit it, Charlie," Reeve pressed. "You knew the piece was stolen from a museum, and you still went along with the deal."

Now Clea understood, and she was afraid that Reeve was right. Glancing at her brother, she saw that he was going to offer no denial.

Charlie had raised himself up in bed—or attempted to—coughed, and laid back down, trying to deny what was obvious to everyone: Reeve was on to him. "Okay," he acquiesced, "let's say I'm savvy enough to know that carvings like the jade jaguar don't grow on trees, but until I made the deal, I didn't actually know the details. Then it was too late to pull away. Hell, if I'd backed out I'd probably be dead now. So let's call the whole scam an error in judgment."

"A serious one," Reeve agreed as he moved away from the bed, stopping beside Clea. "I imagine you'll want to stay here in Santa Inez with Charlie until he recovers. I'll meet you at the hotel with your luggage."

Reeve walked to the door, turning one last time to look at Charlie. "As for you, old pal, stay in the hospital as long as you can; it's better than jail."

"Reeve," Clea called out as she started to follow him.

Charlie's plea stopped her. "Don't walk out on me now, Sis."

"I should, Charlie," she said, feeling defeated.

"Please, Sis." He reached for her, and she took his hand.

"Listen, Clea, I know I was wrong and stupid, but if they connect me with this stolen jade, I could go to jail. I could die there. It's happened before. Surely, you don't want that."

"Of course I don't, Charlie."

"If you could help me just this one time, I swear—"

"Charlie." Her voice sounded her hopelessness. There'd been too many last times for Charlie. But what was she to do?

"I know. I've said it before, but this time I mean it. I'm scared, really scared. If we can just verify where the jade is, then we can find a way to get it back somehow. I know we can." There was desperation in his eyes. "I'll do anything to get out of this, Clea."

"Even start telling the truth?"

"Even that." Charlie tried to smile. "There're some things I've never lied about, and you know it. I love you, Clea, and I respect Reeve more than anyone I've ever known. I trust him. If he could just prevail on Browning to give the statue back—"

"Charlie, Reeve has done all he's going to do. He's gone. Don't you understand? He isn't going to help you any more." Somehow that gave Clea a feeling that was even deeper than despair over Charlie's situation. She felt the emptiness for herself, too.

"Maybe not," Charlie said. "You could talk to him."

"How do you think I got him to come in the first place, Charlie?" Clea was getting angry now. "I convinced him to bring me to you. That's all he promised; that's all he's going to do."

"He's my only hope, Clea."

Clea felt herself shiver with fright, knowing Charlie was right.

"Go to him again. Ask him to find Browning and check him out for me. You have to make Reeve change his mind. Please." He clutched Clea's hands tightly.

Before she left the room, Clea knew she would do what her brother asked even if Reeve turned her down, even if he walked away from her again—for good. She had to do it for Charlie.

REEVE WAS WAITING FOR HER at the door of the hospital. "I thought—" she began.

"I wasn't going to leave you here alone at night, Clea," Reeve said, taking her arm and leading her down the stairs to the street. "I'm taking you back to the hotel. After that, you're on your own—you and Charlie."

5

"I'LL MAKE SURE you're settled at the hotel and then leave tomorrow," Reeve told her as they traced their steps through the cavernous hospital building.

Clea let herself be led out into the early evening air where the usual line of taxis waited at the curb. They took the first one.

"Thanks for waiting," she said, "but you don't have to stay over."

"I know that," he replied almost sharply as he leaned forward and told the driver to take them to the docks. "You can pick up your things, check into the hotel, then we can have dinner. You are planning to stay, aren't you?" he asked, turning to Clea.

"I'd like to, but I know that leaves you without a crew."

"No problem," he said easily. "There're always guys at the docks who want to crew back to California."

"Then I guess it's all settled." She tried to dismiss her sudden feeling of abandonment.

"Let's get you to the hotel." He was all business now. "Is the White Dove all right with you?"

"I suppose so. It's pleasant, convenient—"

"And money is no object," he finished for her.

Clea didn't respond, but she couldn't help wondering if his sarcasm was covering deeper feelings. Certainly, he wanted nothing more to do with Charlie's problems, but did he really want to dispose of her so summarily just as the friendship was beginning again? Judging from his next remark, he obviously wanted exactly that.

"I'll call the hotel from the dock and make your reservation."

"Thanks," she said with as little rancor as possible. They'd reached the dock and while Reeve paid the driver she got out, heading for the boat one last time.

CLEA GLANCED AT HER WATCH. Seven o'clock and she was almost ready. She gave her reflection in the mirror one last inspection. She'd wanted to look her best, perhaps because it would be their last night together or perhaps just for her own pride, hoping that when he left the memory of her would stay with him.

Unfortunately, she wasn't prepared to make much of an impression. She'd neglected to bring anything dressy on the trip. She rummaged through her clothes and found a black T-shirt and unearthed a white cotton skirt from the bottom of her duffel bag. Further searching turned up a hot pink belt, which she pulled off of a pair of shorts. That was the outfit; it would have to do.

After washing and drying her hair, Clea decided to let it fall to her shoulders and added a pair of lime-green earrings. If not exactly California chic, the look was a little wild and funky. She liked it but had no idea what Reeve's reaction would be. At this point it didn't really matter; still, she was curious.

He was sitting on the patio waiting for her. She paused at the arched doorway so that she could observe him without being seen. She'd meant to be an uninterested onlooker, but to Clea's chagrin she felt the accelerated beating of her heart brought on by no more than the first glimpse of Reeve.

He was leaning against the bar, one foot on the rail with a casualness that was entirely natural, totally unaware of the way his cotton twill pants fit snugly, wrinkling across the crotch then smoothing out over his thighs. He had one hand in his pants pocket; the other held a glass of wine. His light blue polo shirt delineated the smooth lines of his chest and shoulders. His hair was damp and brushed back from his face, and Clea imagined he'd just taken a shower.

She followed his gaze and saw that he was watching a young couple who'd come onto the patio and were standing near the bar, arms entwined, lips a fraction apart, whispering and laughing.

Clea watched them enviously, just as Reeve seemed to, and tried not to think of that time when the two of them had been like these lovers, oblivious to everyone and everything. Taking a deep breath she closed her eyes for a moment and rid herself of the young couple's happiness. Then, eyes focused ahead, she moved down the stairs toward the bar.

He turned to her immediately as if he'd anticipated her arrival. Clea thought she read pleasure on his face. His words confirmed her thoughts.

"Clea, you look sensational. How did you manage to put together that outfit from one innocent-looking duffel bag?"

Clea sank onto the bar stool beside Reeve, glowing from his praise but not about to tell him of the time and effort involved. "After years of travel, I suppose I've learned to pack efficiently. You never know when you might have a night on the town at the best hotel." She met his eyes with a smile.

"I gather your accommodations here are to your liking?"

"Definitely," Clea told him.

"And you're determined to stay?"

"At least until Charlie gets out of the hospital. I'm sure you can understand that I don't want him taken off to jail, Reeve."

"If that's going to happen, I can't imagine that you can prevent it, Clea."

"I can try," she responded adamantly if somewhat uneasily.

"Yes, you can," he agreed before changing the subject. "But not now, not tonight. This is our evening, and we're going to enjoy it," he declared, taking her hand. "Come on, let's get a good table with a view and order a spectacular dinner. We've proven ourselves and we deserve a treat."

After they were seated and Reeve had ordered a margarita for Clea, she picked up on his last remark. "What did you mean by proven ourselves?"

"Well." Reeve leaned forward. "We undertook this quest for two reasons—one to see what we could do to help Charlie, and the answer to that is not one damned thing; the other to reestablish our friendship, and we've done just that. You've been a good sport, a real trouper."

"But what have we proven?" Clea persisted.

"Exactly what you said we could, Clea, that old antagonisms could be put away and replaced by a new friendship."

Clea tried to hide a nagging feeling of disappointment at his words as she took a sip of the icy drink their waiter had delivered. If Reeve's words weren't what she'd wanted in her heart to hear, at least he'd given her the opening to keep her promise to Charlie.

"The quest isn't over," she said. "We haven't helped Charlie at all."

"We can't help Charlie," Reeve replied as he waved the waiter over. "I understand the lobster is brought in fresh twice a day?"

The waiter nodded with a smile. "Best in all Santa Inez."

"We'll have two large."

"Reeve—" Clea attempted.

"You'll eat it all. I guarantee."

He was right. Hungrier than she'd realized after their eventful day, Clea attacked the lobster with enthusi-asm.

"See, I told you," Reeve said as he watched with a smile.

Dinner was over and they were drinking their coffee when Clea returned to the subject of Charlie, taking a different tack this time.

"I can understand why you'd be angry at him and want to walk away. I'm angry, too."

"But you can't walk away."

"He's family, Reeve, the only brother I have—right or wrong."

"Bailing him out only increases the dependency, Clea, and—" Reeve stopped in midsentence, shaking his head. "We've had this conversation before. You know how I feel about the tangled web that holds the Moore family together."

"I do, and you're right—and wrong. There's nothing the matter with family ties and having someone to rely on. It's just that Charlie and I take it to the extreme; he in rebelling and I in conforming, although I'm trying to change."

At Reeve's skeptical look, she went on, "I guess Charlie and I need to learn something, take a little from each other's style. I believe Charlie's ready to do that now. He's scared, Reeve."

"I don't blame him. He should be."

"Not just of jail," Clea added, "but of my family finding out. This would kill my mother."

Reeve drained his coffee cup. "You can't go through life basing all your decisions on whether you're going to please or upset your parents, Clea. At some point you have to live your life for yourself."

"All of us aren't selfish enough to do that," she said tartly.

Reeve smiled at the intended barb. "You're right. I am selfish, and on my one night in Santa Inez with my newfound friend I don't want to talk about her brother."

Clea made one last-ditch effort. "Well, if you would change your mind and go to Denver, I'd go with you. I could help, you know."

"That's a nice offer, Clea, but we both know we've come to the end of the line. Neither of us is going to Denver."

Clea finished her coffee. "I don't know about that. I might just go by myself and find out about this man Browning," she said slyly.

Reeve frowned then said seriously as if trying to convince himself, "I'm sure you have more sense than to try that, Clea. Look what Browning did to Charlie. You're much too beautiful to end up bruised and battered in the hospital."

Clea looked up sharply. "Don't patronize me, Reeve."

Reeve reached across the table for her hand. "I'm not patronizing you, but I'm still being selfish. Now, very selfishly, I'd like to dance with you. The band sounds pretty good." He stood up, still holding onto her hand.

The band that had begun playing during dinner was swinging into dance tunes, and several couples were on the floor. Clea stood and followed Reeve, surprised that he wanted to dance, excited at the prospect of being in his arms again.

Reeve was surprised himself that he'd asked her to dance. It was a dangerous move. He knew that, but he justified it by reminding himself that it would be his last chance to hold her.

As they reached the dance floor she smiled at him, and Reeve thought about the sail down the coast. She'd worked very hard, and he'd allowed little time for them to be close. And even though he'd be staying overnight on the boat, he'd moved her to the hotel, once more avoiding closeness.

The moment she reached up to put her hand on his shoulder and he took her in his arms, Reeve knew why he'd avoided it. It was too tempting, being this near her. A moment like this together on the boat, and he wouldn't have been able to stop himself from making love to her—as he'd wanted to do from the beginning.

Now she was in his arms, her body close, fitting into his just as he'd remembered, but this was safe, Reeve reminded himself. They were in public.

Yet he didn't feel all that safe as her firm breasts molded against his chest, her abdomen against his hips, her blond head settled just beneath his chin. This was dangerous territory.

Reeve's hand was meant to be at her waist, holding her gently against him as they swayed to the music. He forced himself to keep it there although he wanted to slide it upward along her spine to the softness of her neck and then down, around the fullness of her hips as he pulled her even closer.

Reeve kept his hand where it was, but the thought of what he *could* do, made his heart beat faster. His skin was damp despite the cooling breeze blowing across the patio. He could hear his breath catch deep in his throat and wondered if Clea noticed what she was doing to him, how just holding her was setting him on fire.

Reeve knew that he should take her back to the table, say good-night and walk away. Instead, he kept on dancing.

"This music's just perfect," Clea said softly, breaking the spell of Reeve's fantasy.

He nodded; that was all he could do.

Clea didn't notice anything except how wonderful it felt to be in Reeve's arms again. She fit so well there, as if she belonged. She always had; that much would never change. The comfort of being held by Reeve—the steady beating of his heart, the clean scent of his aftershave and the crispness of his collar against her hand—was mixed with the fantasy that they were young and in love and this night would last forever.

Then the music stopped. Reeve stepped away and reality took over. He was leaving tomorrow; their journey was ended. That filled her with a longing almost too intense to bear.

"The band's taking a break," he said in a voice that seemed to come from far away. "Shall we call it a night, too?"

Clea nodded. Her heart was too full to speak. She didn't want the night to end, but there was no way to hold on to it.

Reeve put his hand under Clea's elbow and walked her off the dance floor to their table. There he carelessly counted out a few bills and dropped them beside the check. Then they walked out together, past the patio, crossing the cool tiled floor of the lobby to the wide stairway that led to her room. Clea had no idea what he was thinking. She only knew that he would soon be gone, back to California, out of her life again.

At her door, Clea fumbled in her bag for the oversize key, which he took from her to insert in the lock. It wasn't easy because his hand was shaking, but no more than hers. She looked at him, trying to blink back the tears that clouded her eyes. She meant to thank him for coming with her, but she couldn't speak. Instead, she touched him, putting her hand against his cheek.

"Don't leave," she whispered. "Please."

The sweet moment when their lips met was all he had lived for, Reeve thought as he tasted her soft, moist mouth for the thousandth time and yet for the first time. It was giving, yielding to his, and he demanded all he knew she was ready to give as her arms wrapped around his waist and pulled him closer.

He was free now, released from the agony of the past few days, free to kiss her and not think of the consequences. How could he think, when his blood pounded in his brain and his senses flamed with her? He kissed her long and hard, letting his tongue insinuate deeply into her mouth to be met in its explorations by her own.

They were drawn into her room where the door closed behind them, and their world was created anew. Starving for each other, as desert survivors for water, they clung tightly, their kisses almost desperate, as if in some way they could make up for all the years they'd lost.

Brazenly, Clea returned his kisses, letting a moan escape as she moved her mouth deliriously against his.

Her blood was singing in her veins, pounding in her body, sending messages of need that she knew couldn't be denied.

He was all Clea remembered and more. The warmth of his mouth, the strength of his arms, the taste and touch and scent of him. A dizzying rush of pleasure pulsed through her, taking her breath away and weakening her knees.

Reeve caught her and held her even closer, whispering, "I want to make love to you, Clea. I want that more than anything in life."

As if she were weightless, Reeve scooped her up and carried her to the bed where he lay beside her. His lips had never left hers, and Clea clung to him now, feeling a sudden strength return to her.

As Reeve's hands greedily roamed her body—gliding up the smoothness of her leg, caressing her thigh, sliding over the silkiness of her panties and back again—she held him close.

Their clothes were a torment, a barrier keeping them apart, and together they struggled to shed them. Then there was nothing between them—no barriers, no impediments—only the hunger that wouldn't be denied.

Reeve pulled her close, devouring her mouth again and again as she pressed her eager body against his. Then he drew his lips away from hers and moved downward, leaving a damp trail across her jawbone, down her neck to her breast where he caught the taut pink bud of her nipple between his teeth and bit down gently, causing Clea to cry out in ecstasy.

It was heaven—it was torture, feeling him teasing and tantalizing her so, sending ripples of pleasure all the way down to the tips of her toes. Just when she felt she could stand no more, he moved his hands down her body to caress the secret moist center of her need, and the blissful agony began again.

Clea found his manhood waiting for her, hard and yet silky soft beneath her questing fingers. She slipped her hands around him murmuring words of endearment—words long unspoken—unhesitatingly voicing her need.

"I can't wait, Clea" he murmured. "I want you so much."

"I want you, too, Reeve. Now and always." It was true. She'd never stopped wanting him. Eagerly, she guided him inside of her. Hungry hands and mouths explored each other with near madness as their bodies clung fiercely together, taking and giving, meeting each other's demands and yet demanding more and more.

He looked down at her below him, her hair shining on the pillow, her eyes closed, her face a mirror of the ecstasy he felt. He wanted to tell her what those feelings were; he wanted to tell her everything. Instead he called her name again and again. "Clea, Clea . . ."

She arched toward him, and in answer Reeve thrust deeply, again and again, moving with her in a frenzied passion until at last the release came. It was explosive, leaving them clinging to each other, their hearts pounding madly, their bodies damp and slick with the heat of their passion.

Reeve held her tightly until her hot skin grew warm then cool against his. She belonged to him at that moment—all of her. It was a moment he swore he would never forget.

Smoothing her damp hair from her forehead and kissing the soft curve where her temple and hairline met, he tried to tell her his thoughts, but the words wouldn't come. Instead, he held her closer, his heart too full for him to speak.

Looking at him, Clea snuggled even closer and slipped one of her slim legs between his. "Don't leave me, Reeve," she whispered. "Stay with me tonight."

THEY WOKE DURING THE NIGHT and turned to each other again. Slowly and easily, as Reeve had meant for them to make love the first time, they made love in the dark, and it was just as wonderful as before.

JUST BEFORE DAWN Reeve awakened from a fitful sleep. Clea was still curled in his arms, sleeping peacefully with the suggestion of a smile on her lips.

Gently he untangled himself from her arms and slipped out of bed. For a moment he thought she was going to wake up, but after a little sigh her breathing returned to normal.

The sigh stayed with Reeve and bothered him. It was a sigh that had sadness in it as if she knew that he'd slipped away and was leaving.

And he *was* leaving. Pulling on his clothes, he looked down at her again. He was a coward; he knew that, but he was also wise enough to know that words spoken in the heat of passion meant nothing in the glare of morning light.

What had happened between them had been special, and Reeve wouldn't forget it. But their bodies had been in control, not their minds or even their emotions.

It made more sense for him to leave now and let her awaken alone. That would give her time to think about what had happened, and Reeve was sure she'd see it for what it really was—the passions of the past taking hold uncontrollably.

It had been inevitable from the first moment she'd walked onto his boat in Newport, but it could only have happened here in Santa Inez, far away from their real lives. This was a fantasy; beautiful, ephemeral and doomed not to last. The fantasy had come to an end once before; it would again. Except this time Reeve would end it before it really began and both of them got hurt all over again.

Reeve finished dressing and looked down at Clea once more, unable to resist touching her golden hair with one careful hand before turning abruptly and walking out the door.

The morning air was deliciously cool, and it helped to put everything in perspective, clearing his head so that he could warn himself not to take another step in the direction they'd been heading last night; not to get started all over again, tied up in the webs of the Moore family, living the way they wanted him to, meeting their needs. Nothing had changed. Despite Clea's protestations, she was still dancing to her parents' tune; Charlie was in trouble, and Reeve was there for them. He didn't want it; he didn't need it.

Stepping onto the boat, Reeve felt secure again and relieved to be on his own turf. All he had to do was find someone to crew for him and hoist the sails. But as soon as the thought formed, he knew it was useless. He couldn't sail away and leave her.

Even after the lecture he'd given himself, he was going to stay.

He stood in the bow as the sun came up, still trying to change his mind but knowing he wouldn't. If he didn't help, she was determined enough and stubborn enough to go after the jade on her own. The idea was preposterous, but he knew that Clea could convince herself to go to Denver in search of Browning. He couldn't leave knowing she would be in danger. So for Clea, not for Charlie, he'd help out one more time. Then he'd be out of their lives for good; all debts honorably paid.

6

CLEA WOKE UP SLOWLY and reached for Reeve. He wasn't there. She rolled over and opened her eyes, expecting to see him sitting on the side of the bed or standing nearby looking down at her.

The room was empty, his crumpled clothes that had been on the floor beside hers gone. He couldn't just have left without a word, she thought as her mind raced in search of other possibilities.

Maybe she'd dreamed it all, Clea told herself. But she knew better. Her lips were bruised by his kisses, and her entire body glowed with the tingling ache left by his lovemaking. There wasn't an inch of her that he hadn't touched, kissed, left his mark on. It was hardly a dream.

It was real, and so was this—the aftermath. And the reality was harsher than any dream.

Somehow, though, she wasn't surprised. Disappointed, yes, but that would pass. There'd been nothing else for Reeve to do this time but walk away. Clea accepted that.

Then why, she wondered, were the tears building in her eyes? Clea blinked them back, forcing herself to get out of bed and head for the shower. She turned it on cold and let the water pound her into sensibility, washing away those thoughts that kept creeping into her mind; thoughts of the two of them.

The shower didn't help at all even though she stood under it for a long time, letting the water stream down her face to her shoulders and below to all the curves of her body where Reeve had caressed her. Reeve. Everything, even the cold shower that was supposed to bring her to her senses, reminded her of Reeve.

Well, they would have to face each other; that much was certain. Clea didn't expect him to sail away without so much as a word. That wasn't Reeve's style. No, he'd come back with an explanation for his departure.

Clea wanted to hear what he had to say. Maybe that would make it easier for both of them, because whatever his explanation, it would be sensible, and she would have no choice but to accept it. They didn't belong together; they never had.

Yet as Clea pulled on shorts and a shirt and gave her hair one last shake, she remembered the night again and how right it all had seemed. How was he going to explain that away?

CLEA WAS AT A TABLE on the patio, pouring her second cup of coffee, when he appeared. He was wearing dark glasses that effectively hid his eyes. At first, wary of seeing into his thoughts, she felt relief. Then she felt a kind of anger that he didn't seem prepared to face her.

"Good morning," Reeve said. He'd crossed the patio and was standing beside the table looking at her. Dappled sunlight danced on his face and, in the trees above, birds were chirping to each other. It was a beautiful day, a peaceful day, in contrast to the turmoil she felt inside.

"Good morning," Clea echoed. "Please join me. I ordered a big pot of coffee. Thought we'd need it," she added, then wondered why she'd said that. Reversing herself, she determined to stay cool and asked quickly, "Would you like a cup?"

"I sure would," Reeve answered as he pulled up a chair. He didn't remove the glasses, and while he looked handsome, he also looked uncomfortable. Clea said nothing to make it easier for him. Then she realized that her silence was making it difficult for her, as well.

She forged ahead, doing all the talking since he didn't seem inclined to help out. "I ordered pastries and fruit, too. They looked delicious, and I'm actually quite hungry."

Reeve smiled, but he remained distant, almost as far away from her as he'd been that first day on the boat. A cold knot of tension formed in Clea's stomach. What if the night had meant nothing to him?

She could stand what was happening between them because she knew it was inevitable. What she couldn't stand was indifference. It had to have been as special for Reeve as for her. Even though it was over, she needed that reassurance.

Suddenly and boldly, she leaned over and removed his glasses. "I want to be able to see you," she said with no further explanation for her words or the gesture that preceded them.

There wasn't much to see. Even without his glasses, his eyes were unreadable.

Clea sat back, her eyes narrowed. He wasn't going to help. In the awkward silence that followed, she waited, feeling suddenly shy as Reeve took a sip of his coffee.

Finally, he spoke. "About last night, Clea . . ."

The tone of his voice was cool and collected, even brusque. She felt her heart flutter.

"I'm sorry," he said.

"Sorry?" She was confused.

"Let's blame it on the wine and the moonlight. And memories."

Clea's confusion dissolved into anger. If it was over, at least they should be able to admit that it had had some meaning. "Blame?" she questioned. "I don't think either of us was to blame, Reeve. Last night was wonderful." She refused to let him off so easily.

"*You* were wonderful, Clea," he admitted, and she felt a sense of relief.

"But I was wrong and out of line."

So he was going to take the blame. Maybe that's how it should be, Clea thought. Maybe that was the only answer.

Reeve looked away then looked back. That's when she saw pain in his eyes. "We were two people trying to recapture a dream that was never meant to be."

"Yes," she agreed. What else could she do; he was right. "We should have enough sense to let it end here."

"Yes," he repeated. "To leave it alone."

"And yet there were some good times in the past," she said, unable to give up what was left of her dream.

"Past is the operative word. It *is* past. Some of it was good, yes, but I can't forget the tough times. I wish I could." He paused for a moment. "Last night was just a logical conclusion to the trip down here."

"Logical conclusion," she echoed sadly.

"I don't mean to make it sound so clinical, but after we got over our initial awkwardness, we worked together and became friends of a sort. Then we—"

"Went to bed," she finished for him. "That's the logical conclusion you were talking about?"

"Don't make it tough on us, Clea."

"I'm trying not to," she told him.

He took her hand and held it for just a moment. "I know."

Clea wasn't sure which of them pulled away first, but quickly the hand-holding was over.

"Happy endings are only in books; not in real life," Reeve said. "We'd both be fools to take the chance that things could work out between us and then get hurt again. It's best just to leave it alone."

Clea nodded.

"Still friends, I hope?"

Clea sipped her coffee, cold and bitter now as the day had become, even as her heart had become. "Friends? Sure," she said with a smile.

"Clea," he began, then faltered.

"What, Reeve?" She was forcing him now, and she knew it, but she couldn't stop. This was his decision, really and, even if she agreed with him, somehow she wanted Reeve to take responsibility. After all, if it had been up to her alone, it might not have ended like this.

"I didn't mean to hurt you. You're the last person in the world I'd ever want to hurt."

"I know that." It was only half an answer; she hadn't let him off the hook, and they both realized it.

Clea took a deep breath and struggled to get her composure back. Then she reached for her own dark glasses so she, too, could hide the feelings that were apparent in her eyes, as Reeve had done. First he'd hidden behind the glasses, then somehow behind a cloud of what appeared to be indifference. She could only hope that was a pose.

"You're right about everything," she said. "We're both older now with a lot more emotional baggage to drag around. And you still don't like the Moore family."

"Present company excluded," he remarked. But the cloud was still there, and she couldn't read the feelings behind his words—if there were any.

The waiter brought the fruit and pastries, and Clea took a roll, which she pulled apart, knowing she couldn't eat it. "I guess you'll be leaving today," she said. "Any luck finding a crew?"

"It doesn't matter."

Clea looked up at him, frowning.

"I'll be leaving, but not on the *Argosy*," he clarified.

She waited, confused, for him to explain.

"I've decided to look into the Denver thing for Charlie."

"Oh, Reeve, that's wonderful." Clea breathed a huge sigh of relief. Just when she was sure she knew what was going on with Reeve, he surprised her again. Then an awful thought hit her, and Clea knew she was going to have to ask. "Is this somehow my reward for last night?"

"No!" he said adamantly. "Don't ever think that, Clea. What happened between us had nothing to do with Charlie."

For a long moment there was silence, then Reeve explained. "Last night did bring back memories for me, wonderful ones of when we were together. Then when we broke up . . ." He shrugged. "But I think I knew all along that it was right for me to finish this out. I came here at your insistence to find Charlie and get to the bottom of his troubles. But it's not over yet, and I can't leave it dangling."

She waited, knowing there was more.

"Besides, I didn't want you going off to Denver."

"I wasn't—"

"Yes, you were, Clea. Admit it. If I had left tomorrow on the *Argosy*, you would have gone to Denver in search of the mysterious Browning."

That was true, but there was more. "I'd still like to go," Clea said.

"Oh, no."

"Reeve—"

"No, Clea. Rest on your laurels. You talked me into this trip, then you talked yourself onto my boat."

She couldn't help smiling.

"Just settle for two out of three. You can stay here or fly back to L.A."

"I'll stay with Charlie," she said, knowing better than to argue at this point.

"If I find out anything in Denver, I'll call you." Reeve didn't expect the trip would turn up any useful information, but there was no need to tell that to Clea or to Charlie. They had it in their heads that Browning was the only solution to Charlie's problems. "Agreed, Clea?" he asked, needing confirmation.

"Agreed," she said, standing up to leave. "Finish your breakfast while I check the airline ticket office. I imagine there're several flights every day since this is a pretty popular tourist spot. I'll see what's available for tonight. The sooner the better, right?"

"I can call later," he said.

"Please, Reeve. Let me. It's the least I can do. Besides," she added, "my Spanish is better than yours." She smiled the old Clea smile, and Reeve felt a little easier about what had happened between them. They still could be friends.

Reeve chose a warm roll and spread it with marmalade. "Okay," he agreed. "Afterward we'll pay the invalid a visit and see what else we can learn about

Browning. I'll need more information before I take off on this—"

"Don't say 'wild-goose chase,'" Clea said with a laugh.

"Expedition," Reeve finished.

"Sounds better," Clea said as she got up with a glance at her watch. "The reservation may take a while. I'll meet you in Charlie's room at the hospital in an hour or so."

"Fine," Reeve said. "See you there."

He watched her retreating back, relieved that she was taking it well. He'd expected a terrible scene when he told her she couldn't go to Denver. It hadn't come, and now he was beginning to realize why. After the way he'd talked about last night, she probably didn't want to be with him ever again.

Reeve bit into the roll. Yet she'd agreed with him about everything. It almost seemed as if it had all been her idea. He thought back over their very complicated conversation. It was a mutual decision, he remembered—a decision they both knew was right.

Wasn't it? Reeve couldn't be sure of anything now. He only knew that the memory of last night was with him and would remain with him forever. He closed his eyes for a moment and let himself remember how she felt and smelled and tasted. He sighed deeply. No matter what he'd said to Clea, those memories would remain precious to him.

Reeve finished the roll without really tasting it. She hadn't been able to eat, and now he didn't seem to be able to, either. He looked around, and all the sights and sounds of the patio came back to him. Funny, Reeve thought, that they'd been sitting there talking for half an hour, and he hadn't even been aware of the surroundings. It had all disappeared when Clea was there. Nothing else had mattered but her.

WHEN HE GOT TO THE HOSPITAL, Reeve went directly to Charlie's room without stopping to check in. Stepping through the door he saw that the light of day had brought some changes. The young man who'd occupied one of the beds was gone, and the old man was asleep. All the activity in the room was in Charlie's corner. As usual. Reeve leaned against the door jamb and watched.

A nurse was taking Charlie's temperature, but he was making the task impossible; in fact, he seemed to be flirting. The nurse was young and rather pretty, even in her nun's habit. She turned and saw Reeve watching, finished her task quickly and left the room. Reeve could have sworn she was blushing.

"Even the nuns, Charlie?" he asked with disbelief.

Charlie grinned. "All women like compliments, and a little fun doesn't hurt anyone," he defended. "Besides it makes my day go by faster. It's pretty boring here, Reeve."

Reeve avoided the desire to remind Charlie that the boredom was a result of his own bad judgment, if not stupidity.

"I envy you, being able to get out of here."

Once more Reeve didn't respond, although Charlie seemed to be waiting for a lecture.

"Going home sounds pretty good to me."

"Except I'm not going home yet," Reeve said, responding at last.

"Oh, did you pick up a charter?" There was something hopeful in Charlie's voice, as if he were still clinging to the possibility that Reeve was going to help him out.

"I think you're aware of what's happening, Charlie. I'm going to Denver."

Charlie's face lit up.

Reeve didn't let the glow last. Not wanting Charlie to think he'd won any kind of battle, he added quickly, "Even though I personally think you ought to be in jail."

"Reeve, don't say that," Charlie warned, looking panicked.

"It's true, Charlie, if not for this recent episode, certainly for your past actions. I'm doing this for—"

"Clea," Charlie interrupted. "I know that. It's for her, not for me."

"Partly," Reeve admitted. "If I don't go, she might take off on her own and get in all kinds of trouble."

"I know; I'd thought of that," Charlie admitted, "but I didn't know what to do about it."

"Well, I know what to do." There was a long pause before Reeve added, "To be honest, I'm also going because I owe you."

Charlie raised an eyebrow.

"You know why," Reeve said. "You came through when I needed the money for the *Argosy*. You never questioned me but just handed it over. For that I owe you, pal."

"Money's easy," Charlie said seriously. "Friendship is another matter." Then some of Charlie's humor returned. "Let's admit it, old pal. You've come through for me many times. You're one of the good guys and always have been. You just can't help yourself."

Reeve ignored the compliment. "Whatever the reason, I'm going to Denver."

"And no matter the reason, I'm grateful."

"So," Reeve said, "let's get down to the nitty-gritty. Tell me about this Browning character."

"He did me in."

"Charlie," Reeve said, getting exasperated. "I realize that. But give me the facts; how you met him, what his life is like? I need something to help me connect with him."

"All right," Charlie replied, making himself as comfortable as possible in the hospital bed. "He's a hard hitter in the stock market. Made lots of money on investments in penny stocks, soybean futures, pork bellies, that sort of stuff. As the money rolled in, he began to upgrade his life-style with a big fancy house in Denver. Found himself a new young wife, got in with the jet set, that whole bit."

Reeve listened without comment. This was the gravy. He'd have to wait for Charlie to get down to what mattered.

"He became a collector," Charlie said.

Now they were getting somewhere, Reeve thought.

"He bought Impressionist paintings like they were going out of style, antiques, pre-Columbian artifacts. And jade. He began to get a reputation as one of the important jade collectors."

"Ah," Reeve said. "But how did he hear about you?"

"He didn't. I heard about him. I keep up with the high rollers, Reeve, through friends, gossip, the press. The word gets out. When I got wind of this deal in Santa Inez, I immediately thought of Browning. I knew he was the one to buy the jaguar. He had the interest, and better yet he had the money. So I made a phone call, using an assumed name of course."

"Why?" Reeve questioned.

"He could have known my old man. The moneyed world is a very small one, Reeve. They all know each other."

"Of course," Reeve said, not without some sarcasm. "So you bought the stolen piece from your contact and went after Browning."

"Exactly. I reached him easily, but I couldn't convince him to come to me. Instead, he sent his representatives. You know the rest."

Reeve nodded. "The representatives took the jade and proceeded to beat you to a pulp."

"I guess that's how the rich get rich. And the poor stay poor," Charlie added. "Anyway, when I could finally use the phone, I called Browning. He said his men hadn't been able to locate me. He was terribly sorry about what happened, the loss of the jade and of course my little problem. Oh, he was a prince, but I could tell he was lying through his teeth. He has the jade, Reeve. I know it, and if we can prove—"

Reeve had stopped listening and was looking out the window to the grounds below. The courtyard had an Old World charm that was surprising. Reeve watched as patients walked or maneuvered wheelchairs over the cobblestones and along paths through the garden. Then something else caught his eye—a man trying to meld into the scenery but not succeeding. There was something in his stance that bothered Reeve, something unnatural, a watchful tenseness. Reeve shook his head. The police seemed to be everywhere.

"You don't make it easy, Charlie," he said finally.

"I guess I never did." Charlie's infectious devil-may-care grin had returned.

Reeve looked away from the window toward the hospital bed where Charlie lay. He was wearing a pair of old pajamas with the top open to reveal his bronzed chest. Even with the bandages, the cast, the leg in traction, he looked like a man who was on top of the world. That was Charlie's trouble, Reeve thought. His looks were so deceiving.

"Some things are going to have to change," Reeve told him, aware that Charlie was listening intently. "I'm not speaking for myself, Charlie. I'll be in and out of this very quickly, but someone else is involved. It's time you stopped thinking about yourself for a change and gave some thought to Clea."

"I owe a lot to her."

"Damn right you do, pal," Reeve replied, exasperated. "She was always there for you, even during our Navy days. How many times would you have been AWOL if Clea hadn't put you back together after a binge and sent you off to San Diego? She even drove you back to the base once, if I recall."

Charlie nodded. "I remember. You pulled duty that weekend and I went up to L.A. alone."

"And got into a scrape, right?"

"Frankly, I don't remember that part. Whatever happened, Clea came through."

"Yeah, you owe her."

"And *you* still care about her," Charlie said.

It was a statement, not a question, and Reeve managed to avoid a direct response. "If *you* care, then you'll give her a break. Let her get on with her life and quit playing baby-sitter for you."

"I don't mean to involve her."

"But you always do, Charlie. It wasn't fair to call her. A plea from you is all it takes. Asking her to find me put Clea in a very uncomfortable position. This has been tough on both of us."

Real consternation showed on Charlie's face. "I thought maybe, I was hoping—"

"That you could get us back together? I can't believe you're really that naive, but maybe you are." Reeve looked out the window then back at Charlie. "Obviously you are. At least Clea and I have been able to salvage a friendship out of all this. For that I thank you."

Afraid he was revealing too much, Reeve added, "But that's all there is to it. Your family would be as adamant about me now as they were then, and neither you nor Clea has learned to handle them."

"Tell me about it," Charlie replied. "At least I've fought them," he continued, a bit apologetically.

"You've rebelled," Reeve corrected. "I don't know how much standing up to them and talking about your disagreements you've done. Very little, I imagine."

Charlie's silence was the answer.

"You just go off on some damned fool escapade," Reeve reminded him. "The more you rebel against them and react to them, the less you act on your own. So you get into one scrape after another, blaming your family then asking to be bailed out. For once I wish you'd forget about your parents and do what's right for you." Reeve broke off, irritated at himself for becoming so impassioned.

"Do what's right," Charlie repeated. "That's the way you've always played it, huh? Straight."

"I try to, but I also make mistakes." Reeve thought about last night. "I'm not a saint, but I try. What about you?"

"I can't make promises, Reeve. I'd only be lying to both of us. All I can do is think about what you've said."

"Fair enough," Reeve replied. It wasn't his problem, after all.

Then another voice interrupted. "Well, you two seem very serious." Clea was standing in the doorway, her gaze directed away from Reeve toward her brother. She looked cheerful, but she was definitely avoiding him.

Clea crossed to Charlie's bed. "We were just talking about Denver," Charlie said as she bent to kiss the portion of his cheek that was visible through the bandages.

"I'm so glad Reeve is going," she said, still not looking directly at Reeve. "But I've been wondering about the jaguar. Do you think Browning will actually have such a priceless piece on view in his living room?"

Charlie shrugged, then winced a little from the effort. "You know about collectors, Clea. They like to keep their acquisitions in the house. Maybe not in the living room, but somewhere. The temptation to show them off is greater than the need to hide them away."

"That's true of legitimate collectors, but the jaguar is stolen—"

"I doubt if it's the only piece that he came by less than honestly," Reeve interrupted, "and his jet-set friends probably know all about it and don't care. You must know that the rich and super-rich have all sorts of masterworks illegally squirreled away." Reeve hadn't been able to keep the slightly condescending tone from his voice, but Clea seemed not to notice.

"The problem is," Reeve went on, "finding one particular piece. A jade jaguar. Can you describe it, Charlie?"

"Well, it's about this high." Charlie tried to indicate the size with his free right hand. "Four and a half, maybe five inches."

"Pretty small to cause such a fuss," Reeve muttered.

Clea ignored him and fished in her purse for a pad and pencil, which she handed to Charlie. "Draw it for Reeve."

"This'll be tough, but maybe you can figure it out." He worked awkwardly, and then handed the sketch to Reeve.

"It's half man and half jaguar," Charlie explained as Reeve examined the sketch. "The eyes and nose are human, but the lower part of the face tapers into a snout with a thick upper lip. The sides are turned down in a kind of sneer, and the fangs are pretty fierce looking. It has the upper body of a man—real athletic though, with heavy shoulders and haunches. The feet are clawed."

Reeve passed the sketch to Clea who studied it carefully. "Not something I'd like to meet on a dark night in the woods," she said.

"You know about art, Clea. Can't you tell it's Olmec?" Charlie asked.

Clea shook her head. "The jaguar was a common theme among the Indians of Mexico," she said. "There could be a slew of these around, maybe not Olmec but certainly Mayan. Browning could very well have others less valuable."

"You can tell this one easily," Charlie assured her. "The jade has a bluish tinge, and there're glyphs on it that look like writing. I can't remember exactly," he said as Clea returned the sketch to Reeve, "but one looks something like a tortoise, and the other has the beak of a large bird."

"Too bad you don't have a photo," Reeve said, pocketing the sketch, "but I'll do the best I can. To tell the truth, I don't hold out much hope for success."

"You underrate yourself," Charlie answered.

"We'll see," said Reeve noncommittally. "Did you make the reservation, Clea?"

She smiled and nodded. It was the first time she'd looked at him directly.

"Then I'll say goodbye, Charlie." Reeve put out his hand. "Try to avoid any more trouble."

Charlie laughed. "As long as I'm in here, that'll be easy. Good luck, Reeve. I'm counting on you." He gave a thumbs-up, which Reeve did his best to ignore.

7

CLEA AND REEVE stepped from the museum into the sun, shielding their eyes from the afternoon glare. Almost simultaneously, they reached for dark glasses, laughing as they descended the stairs to the street.

It had been Clea's idea to stop there so that Reeve could familiarize himself with the Olmec period, but she'd been amazed at the scope of the museum's collection. The long halls were lined with cases of artifacts, and each room was devoted to pre-Columbian statues and stelae.

Inside, it had been shadowy and quiet—the treasures illuminated by soft lights that reflected off intricately carved jade and serpentine, elaborate masks and huge stone monoliths. Clea had walked through the building at Reeve's side, explaining the collection to him, feeling now and then as if they were tourists exploring the unknown together—lovers, maybe even honeymooners. It was a good feeling, and it permeated the walls of the museum and the walls of her mind, as well.

Once in the sunlight the feeling was gone. They had only been researchers, she reminded herself, studying a civilization that for Reeve meant finding the jade carving and getting Charlie out of trouble.

As they walked along, they talked about what they'd seen.

"Olmec, Aztec, Mayan, Toltec—" Reeve clutched his head in mock confusion. "It's too much for me, and to think Santa Inez's one and only museum could be so complete."

"It's a fine collection," Clea agreed. "The director has been diligent in scouring the country for his acquisitions."

Siesta time was over, and the streets were becoming alive with activity as merchants opened their shops and tourists began their daily search for bargains. "I'm glad to know the hefty tourist tax they're all paying is used for something worthwhile like that collection," Reeve said. Then he added as he looked up and down the street, "It's certainly not used for transportation. Not a taxi in sight."

"I'd rather walk anyway," Clea answered. "Maybe I can get some good photographs. If I go for more than three days without shooting something, I have withdrawal symptoms," she joked.

Reeve fell in beside her, still talking about the museum and Charlie's botched-up get-rich scheme. "It must have been an inside job," he mused. "The security in there looked pretty good with all the cases locked and guards stationed everywhere. I'll bet Charlie's contact worked inside."

"He's probably in Acapulco now living it up on what Charlie paid for the jaguar," Clea commented.

"I'm sure he did leave town," Reeve agreed. Then he shook his head. "Criminals or not, I have a great deal of respect for experts in the field. We spent a long time in the museum, and you were very patient with me, but I still doubt if I can tell an Olmec carving from a Mayan. It's going to be difficult to pass myself off to Browning as an expert."

Clea shot him a veiled glance. "Then we'll have to think of another cover." Shaking her head in dismay, she went on. "It's too bad Charlie had to buy a stolen Olmec piece. I mean, it's bad enough that it was stolen, but Olmec—"

Reeve laughed. "Don't forget, our Charlie is a connoisseur."

Clea had slowed down at a narrow street that was no more than an alley. She had her camera slung over her shoulder, and as they turned the corner, she removed the lens cap.

A few yards away an old man sat in a straight-backed chair that was tilted against the brick wall. He was smoking a cigarette, which dangled from his bottom lip, dropping ashes down his jacket. An orange-and-white cat sat at his feet, its head resting on the old man's dusty black shoe.

"Great subject for a picture," Reeve said.

"Yes," Clea answered as she walked toward the old man.

"Why don't you just shoot?" Reeve asked. "He's not paying any attention to us."

"No, I always ask unless the action happens so fast there isn't time."

"Well, you have plenty of time for this one," Reeve said with a laugh as he observed the lazy scene that Clea entered, speaking slow and careful in Spanish, making gestures that would explain what her vocabulary lacked.

The old man nodded sleepily, and Clea stepped back, taking a few shots in rapid succession from different angles.

As they walked on, still discussing the Olmecs, Clea kept a lookout for a good composition, stopping once to frame the front of a dilapidated house where a chicken stood just inside the entrance, scratching on the dirt floor. There was more than picture-postcard prettiness to Santa Inez, she was discovering. There was life and vitality and reality, and Clea couldn't resist trying to capture some of it on film.

"It's too bad you couldn't take pictures in the museum," Reeve said.

"I know," Clea agreed, "some of the Olmec work is so sophisticated and stylized, and some so abstract, almost like Picasso."

"It's hard to imagine their civilization dated back to the golden age of Greece, and then they just disappeared off the face of the earth—*if* what you tell me is true," Reeve teased.

Clea, who'd leaned over to take a closeup of some detail on a doorway, paused and looked up at Reeve. "We artists stick to the facts," she said. "One day the Olmecs just vanished—poof—as suddenly as they appeared. Isn't it sad?"

Reeve did feel a pang of sadness, not about any vanished civilization, but about Clea, who'd once longed to sail the seas with camera in hand, searching for adventure. Looking at her now, her face alive with excitement, he saw the girl he'd once known, ready to take on the world. He wished that she could have had her dream.

"Yes, it's sad," he agreed, talking about the Olmecs now. "But they left so much behind. Those carvings were incredible, the gods and demons—half man and half animal, like Charlie's jaguar."

"You have good taste."

"I've always known that," he teased. Again, Reeve wasn't thinking of the carvings but of Clea and the first time he saw her. He'd known then she was something special. Quickly, he pushed the thought away. After today he probably wouldn't see her again, and he was lucky to have this time with her.

She stopped once more, camera ready, and he turned to move out of her way. It was then that he saw a familiar face. He wasn't surprised. Less than a block behind them was the man he'd seen from the window of Charlie's hospital room.

Casually Reeve leaned toward Clea and draped an arm over her shoulder. "Don't turn around," he said, "but I think there's a cop following us."

Curiosity caused Clea to do just what she'd been advised against. She looked around immediately, and her eyes met those of a slender young man in a pale gray suit. The contact was made; there was no avoiding it now. Reeve barely had a chance to whisper before the man came within earshot, "Play it cool, Clea. Don't panic."

"Señorita Moore," the man said in a voice that indicated he would have preferred to avoid the encounter Clea's curiosity had forced upon him.

"Yes?" She fought to keep her voice level.

"I would like to ask you one or two questions, if I may."

"You seem to know my name, *señor*, but I have no idea who you are." Her voice was steady even though her heart pounded like a hammer on an anvil. She could feel the perspiration forming on her palms.

"Señor Jorge Alvarez, Santa Inez Police."

"Police?" Clea feigned surprise, hoping her eyes didn't give her away.

"We will move into the shade, please." It wasn't an order, but he seemed confident they would follow him as he walked toward a bench beneath two straggly palm trees. Clea and Reeve followed but remained standing with Clea clutching Reeve's hand tightly. He seemed so calm to her, and she tried to draw strength from him.

"And you, *señor*, your name, please?" Alvarez asked.

"Reeve Holden, but I expect you know that."

Alvarez didn't answer but his eyes, unusually pale against his swarthy skin, narrowed. "You have enjoyed your visit to the jade collection at the museum?"

Clea started to respond, but Reeve gave her hand a warning squeeze. "I can't imagine you followed us here to ask about our trip to the museum."

Clea felt herself beginning to panic and grasped Reeve's hand more tightly, hoping that the man's mention of jade was accidental, fearing it was not. A sinking feeling invaded the pit of her stomach.

"Perhaps not," Alvarez agreed.

"Then why—" Clea began.

Alvarez answered abruptly. "I will try to clear up the confusion. We have been watching the room of Señor Charles Moore at the hospital. We are interested in who comes to visit him, and you are the first."

Clea felt on safer ground. "Of course I visited him. He's my brother."

"We know that, *señorita*, but we wonder just what *you* know. For example, your brother has been involved in a serious incident here in Santa Inez. Did he speak to you of it?"

Clea realized suddenly that Alvarez was fishing, and decided to take the offensive. "Of course I know, and I'm shocked. The vicious attack on my brother at La Paloma Blanca was scandalous, and it seems to me that nothing has been done about it."

She was satisfied with the reply, which caused Alvarez's face to fill with annoyance. "We are investigating that, but—"

Once again Clea came back with a strong response. "But what? My brother was brutally attacked, and instead of looking for his attackers you're following me, asking about museums."

"*Señorita*, we will conduct the investigation into what happened as we think best. A crime has been committed—"

"It certainly has, and my brother is the victim."

"It is possible that he is more than that, *señorita*," Alvarez said. "We have reason to believe that your brother is involved in the theft of a valuable piece of jade from our museum."

Fighting panic, Clea maintained her determination not to be drawn into a discussion about the jade. "I have no idea what you're talking about. My brother is not a thief but a victim," she insisted. "And you are clearly derelict in your duty."

Alvarez's eyes narrowed again, and Clea felt trapped. It wasn't working, and she didn't know what to do next. That's when Reeve broke in.

"We appreciate the problems of your investigation, Señor Alvarez, but Señorita Moore is concerned only for her brother. I'm sure you can understand that. However, if you are making some accusation against her, perhaps you should do so at the police station."

Clea's stomach gave another lurch at the thought of actually being taken away to the police station. She looked sharply at Reeve, who paid no attention as he continued. "If you have no legal cause to detain us, then we'd like to continue our tour of your lovely city. There is no crime in visiting the sights, including the museum, is there, Señor Alvarez?"

"Of course not," Alvarez replied as Clea's stomach returned almost to normal. "We wish for you to enjoy your stay here in Santa Inez, but I must ask that you report to me whatever you know of the missing jade."

"We know nothing about any jade, Señor Alvarez," Reeve replied. "But we will be sure to keep in touch." With that, Reeve wheeled Clea sharply around and started down the street.

"*Adios, señor,*" Clea managed as she was whisked away.

They walked for several blocks in silence, not looking back, before Clea managed to breathe normally again. "Reeve, that was awful. For a moment I was afraid we really would end up at the police station. Just imagine—"

"I'm trying not to," Reeve said with a half smile, "but I don't think there was ever any danger of that. He doesn't seem to know anything about Charlie and the jade. In cases like this, offense is the best defense, and you did great, Clea."

"Is he still following?" Clea was still a little shaky.

"Yep, but discreetly. Just act like a tourist, and we'll make our way along the waterfront to the hotel."

"I don't suppose we could try to lose him," Clea said, attempting a joke.

"I guarantee they know you're at the hotel," Reeve said, "so let's just keep it simple. That looks like a good photo opportunity coming up ahead. How about kids playing on the dock with boats in the background?"

Clea smiled at him. "Sounds great. I'll have to hire you as a consultant." She'd almost recovered but couldn't help one last observation. "I've never been arrested—or almost arrested."

"I don't think we were even close to arrest. But let's get back to the subject of hiring me as a consultant. That sounds like a good idea."

Clea laughed. "Then look for another setup while I get this shot." She was soon deep in concentration on her work, with thoughts of Alvarez almost blocked from her mind.

Reeve gave a final, longing glance at the *Argosy*, securely lying at anchor. "She ought to be okay for a couple of days," he said.

"I know you're an anxious parent, but the boat will be fine," Clea assured him. "She's safely anchored, and Lord knows you paid the dock-master enough to keep his eye on her."

Reeve laughed then. "Okay, so I worry. Wait one minute, there's just one more line I need to check."

He started to move away, but Clea held on to his arm. "You've checked and rechecked. Reeve. Time is running out. You're packed for the flight, but I'm not ready for our trip to the airport."

"What do you mean, *our* trip? I thought you were staying here to nursemaid Charlie."

"Alone in this city with Señor Alvarez? No way," Clea said with a laugh. "Besides aren't you always telling me to let Charlie grow up?"

"I sure am, Clea, but—"

"Actually Alvarez had nothing to do with my decision," Clea admitted. "I booked my flight to L.A. and yours to Denver. We're leaving about the same time this evening so there's no reason we can't share a cab to the airport, is there?"

"None at all," Reeve agreed. "What about the tickets?"

"Picked them up this morning while you were at the hospital with Charlie. I got the boarding passes, too. Now we're all set if Alvarez will let us leave."

"Don't worry. He'll probably be happy to see us go. Besides, the Santa Inez police don't have the budget to track us to the States."

"Then let's get out of here," Clea said. She headed for the hotel with Reeve beside her, still trying to figure Clea out. Something told him she had plans she wasn't revealing.

"WHAT A RIDE." Clea took a deep breath for the first time since they'd stepped into the airport taxi.

"The driver was determined to get us here on time," Reeve answered, his eyes sweeping the terminal, "and we made it, all right." Reeve noted that his flight to Denver was on time, while Clea had forty minutes to wait for the plane to Los Angeles. "I'd better get to my gate."

"Reeve, wait a minute, please."

This was it, he figured—Clea's last-ditch argument to go with him, the reason she'd arranged their flights so close together. "No, Clea. Your ticket's for L.A., and that's where you're going."

"Maybe I can change it," she began.

"Forget that, Clea. I'm not involving you in this Denver mess."

"He's my brother, Reeve."

"We've been through that, remember?"

"But you're going to Denver so it makes sense for me to—"

"Never."

During their conversation, Reeve's flight was called, but Clea was oblivious, caught up in her own problem. "I can help you in Denver, and you know it."

"I don't know any such thing, and I'm not letting you go with me. It's too dangerous. Please be sensible about this."

"Sensible?" Clea pondered the word. "That's what I'm trying to be, Reeve, by not letting emotions get in the way. I realize that part of your objection to my going with you stems from what happened last night—"

"That has nothing to do with it," he replied, almost too hastily.

Her eyes proved she didn't believe him. "I want to go with you, Reeve. If I thought for one minute that—that last night in some way might keep me from helping him, I couldn't live with it."

"Last night isn't the reason, Clea. It's too damned dangerous for you to continue on this escapade." As Reeve argued, he realized that there was also danger in their being together. In a way, Clea was right. He was afraid of that danger, too.

"We can minimize the danger, if it's real, by working together. Just listen to me, Reeve," she said when he started to object, "we did well on the boat as a team. We can do the same in Denver as long as we concentrate on Charlie's problem and forget about us."

Reeve couldn't refute that argument; but he was tired of arguing. He wasn't letting her go to Denver, and that was that. "I don't need a watchdog, Clea. I'll take care of this on my own." He wanted that to be the final word, and he turned away to make his point, but Clea wouldn't let it die. She reached for his arm.

"Reeve, Charlie and I both think you're the only one who can handle this."

"Then let me do it, Clea, for God's sake."

"But—"

"Ah, there we go," he said, quirking an eyebrow. "You have some doubt."

"Not in you, Reeve. Never. But you don't have a cover. Browning isn't going to let you near his house without a logical excuse. What's it going to be?"

Reeve was getting exasperated, and it showed. "I'll figure that out, Clea. Don't worry about it."

"I have an idea, and using it, we can definitely get in," she tempted.

Reeve didn't want to hear any more. "My plane is boarding in five minutes, Clea."

"Photography," she said, not missing a beat. "I have the credentials, the contacts, the believability. I know the circles these people move in, and I know how to reach them."

"And I don't?"

Clea shrugged.

Reeve realized that Clea had a point. In fact, it was a damned good one, but he still wasn't going to give in. There was double jeopardy in taking her along, and he refused to chance it.

Clea persisted. "We can go to Browning's house on the pretext of shooting a magazine piece. I can have that story corroborated easily enough. Then we'll have the run of the whole place. We can even photograph the jade if it's there."

Reeve had stopped listening. He knew it was a good idea, but he wasn't buying it. "That's the call for my flight, Clea," he said.

"Reeve—"

He checked his ticket and seat assignment. "I have to go." He leaned down and kissed her cheek. "Goodbye,

Clea. I'll do my best, I guarantee you." Then he turned and walked away, trying to ignore the empty feeling inside.

SETTLING IN HIS SEAT, Reeve noted with relief that the space next to him was vacant. At least he wouldn't have to spend time in conversation with a stranger. He missed Clea already, and he was having trouble coming to terms with the idea that he might not see her again. Finally he closed his eyes, leaned back in his seat and tried to avoid thoughts of Clea, wishing life didn't hurt so much.

Reeve felt rather than saw someone settle in the aisle seat just before the engines started up. Deliberately he kept his eyes shut, feigning sleep.

"Excuse me, sir, but your elbow is on my armrest."

His eyes shot open. Clea was beside him.

"I'm not that easy to get rid of." She smiled her gamine's grin.

"Clea, dammit, I should have known you had a trick up your sleeve. In fact, I did know, but I thought the trick was going with me to the airport and trying to change my mind."

"That was part of it."

"I should have had the foresight to check your ticket. Well, you're not getting away with it."

Calmly she fastened her seat belt. "No need to be testy, Reeve. You need me, and my idea is a great one."

"The plane hasn't taken off yet. All I have to do is ring for the attendant," he threatened.

"And all I have to do is make a terrible scene," she countered. "Then we'll both be thrown off."

As she spoke the cabin doors closed and the attendant's voice came over the intercom. "Too late, Reeve," Clea said smugly. "We're on our way to Denver."

"AND THIS IS MADAME'S SUITE." With an officious wave of his hand, the bellboy at the Brown Palace Hotel ushered Reeve and Clea through the door.

"Double bed, bath and dressing room, and of course a sitting room." He indicated the appointments of the suite, which was decorated in pale green and mauve, and drew back the curtains, announcing, "A view of the mile-high city."

Clea nodded and sank down on the bed, exhausted. "It's lovely."

"And the gentleman has an adjoining suite." He gestured toward the doorway to Reeve's room.

"Fine," Reeve said, taking a bill from his wallet, "but it's very late. We can skip the tour."

"And naturally you wish to be alone," the bellboy purred as he pocketed the proffered money and with one last adjustment of Clea's curtains was gone.

"All he needed was a leer and a mustache to twirl," Clea commented.

"He *had* the leer, or didn't you notice?" Reeve asked as he opened the door between their rooms. "You look beat. Is there anything I can get for you?"

"No, thanks. I'm too tired to eat or drink—or even think."

Reeve was silent as he studied her face. In spite of the somewhat humorous episode at the airport in Mexico, dealing with her brother's situation over the past few days couldn't have been easy on Clea. The strain was showing on her face.

"Everything's going to work out," he assured her. "Your plan's a good one, and I think we can pull it off with a minimum of danger to you."

"Then I should make a few calls and get things rolling."

"Tomorrow," he said firmly. "There's no rush. You need to get some sleep, and so do I."

Clea's eyes were already closed.

"Good night," Reeve said softly, but he was pretty sure she didn't even hear him as he shut the door between their rooms and leaned against it. Then, reaching for the lock, he stopped and laughed aloud.

What the hell did he think he'd lock out? His memories of the night in Mexico? His feelings when she'd fallen asleep on the plane, her head on his shoulder, and he'd held her close as if she were a little girl? The way she'd looked just now, so vulnerable and fragile, made him want to take her in his arms and hold her again.

It was one thing to desire a woman. He'd been fighting that battle since they stepped onto the boat, and he'd managed to handle it. But the other feelings, the need to protect her and take care of her, were more powerful and more dangerous. If only he could cradle her in his arms and let her know it was all going to be all right.

But that was for lovers, and they'd both agreed that wasn't where their relationship was going. Clea had made it clear from the outset that this was business and she was here for her brother. With a sigh Reeve headed for the shower, wondering why he seemed so determined to play with lightning when he'd probably get burned again.

REEVE'S ARM was around her waist, holding her near. His shoulder was a comforting pillow for her head. It was bliss just being beside him, her body warm against his. His voice murmured her name as Clea raised her lips for his kiss. She felt his hand on her breast as his mouth grazed hers.

Clea stirred and reached for him, but beneath her hand was nothing but the cool cotton sheet. She opened her eyes then closed them again. She was in bed in her hotel room, alone. Some time during the night she'd gotten up, brushed her teeth, put on a nightgown and fallen back into bed and slept for almost ten hours, only to be awakened by an erotic dream about the man in the room next door.

Reluctantly, she gave up her thoughts of Reeve and opened her eyes. It was nine o'clock. She'd overslept, and yet he hadn't wakened her. Suddenly a terrible thought invaded her mind. Maybe he'd already left for the Browning house. That would be just like Reeve, trying to protect her by doing it alone.

Clea padded over to his door and knocked loudly. There was no answer. She opened the door and peered in. The bed, rumpled, with the covers pulled back, was empty, and there was no sound from the shower. He was gone!

"Damn," she murmured as she headed toward her own bath. She hadn't come this far to be left out.

A few minutes later, Clea stepped out of the shower, her head swimming with ideas on how to track him down. Wrapped in a towel, she went into the bedroom and headed for her suitcase. His voice stopped her.

"Good morning, Clea." Reeve was sitting on the sofa, sipping a cup of coffee. On a tray table in front of him was a carafe of orange juice, a steaming pot of coffee and a plate of sweet rolls. "Won't you join me for breakfast?"

Clea stopped to adjust to the sight of him and pulled the towel closely around her damp body.

"I thought if we had breakfast here we'd have a better chance to go over our plans for the day," Reeve was saying casually.

Without a word Clea dropped into a chair opposite him. "And *I* thought you'd left me," she said pouring a glass of orange juice.

"I wouldn't do that." Reeve studiously avoided looking at her, but he'd already noticed that her skin was moist and dewy, her hair tangled like a golden halo around her head, the towel not quite hiding all she'd meant for it to hide. Reeve couldn't help thinking that she was nothing like the sophisticated woman who'd stepped onto his boat in Newport Harbor. She looked so young and vulnerable that he felt a catch in his heart.

"We have a lot to do today," he said, assuming a businesslike tone in order to slow his racing heart. "Maybe you should get dressed."

"Of course," Clea said, tugging at the towel, very aware of the intimacy of the situation. "It wouldn't do for our friendly bellboy to walk in," she added, attempting a joke. Then, getting quickly to her feet, Clea reached for her bag. "I'll be right back."

That hadn't been smart, she lectured herself as she went into the bathroom to dress. She'd set up just the kind of situation they'd both meant to avoid, but she'd been so glad to see him, so glad that he hadn't taken off alone, that she'd spontaneously joined him without realizing she wasn't wearing a stitch except the towel.

Well, he'd been at fault, too, appearing like that in her room, Clea reminded herself as she ran a brush through her hair. "You sneaked up on me, Reeve," she called out. "Next time you should knock."

"I did, but you were in the shower."

"Knock louder," she advised, stepping into the room. "This," she said, indicating her clothes, "is the best I could do." She was once again wearing the white skirt and black top. "It's okay for warm climates, but not Denver."

"Forget it," Reeve replied. "They'll just think you're an eccentric artist from California."

"If we stay, I'll buy some clothes," she said, sitting down and biting into a roll.

"Let's see if we can get into the Browning house before we begin dressing for success," he warned. "Now, to get down to business, I've done some checking around—"

"Already? Where?"

"Here at the hotel. The desk clerk knows all about Charlie's nemesis. The Brownings have given several parties here and reserved suites for their guests. He's known as a big tipper. He seems well-liked. A pillar of the community."

"So no one will want to believe he's secreted stolen artifacts in his house," Clea determined.

"If indeed he has. All we have now is Charlie's speculation. Another interesting fact is that Browning has a very good relationship with the law in Denver."

"The police?"

"Exactly. Seems he donates heavily to their benevolent societies, participates in drives for underprivileged kids, opens up his mountain retreat for their Christmas parties—"

"In other words," Clea said, "we shouldn't count on the police rushing to our aid if we get in trouble, and they probably won't believe that Browning has done any wrong."

"I'd say you're right about both, but we can still carry out our plan to look around the house and see if Browning has the statue. If he does, we leave the rest to Charlie."

Clea didn't mention that there was very little Charlie could do from a hospital bed. Reeve's commitment to her brother obviously didn't go beyond locating the jaguar. "All right," she said, "I'll call *Trends* magazine. They'll be delighted that I have a free-lance idea, and we'll establish a contact if the Brownings decide to check on us."

"There's one problem," Reeve said. "What about equipment? Aren't we supposed to have tripods and lights and umbrellas, all that paraphernalia?" He was thinking about the equipment in Clea's studio.

"Not for the initial visit. My 35mm camera will be fine for establishing shots. If we need to go back, we can always rent equipment. One thing at a time, Reeve. First we need to get into the house." She went to the phone and dialed the magazine in Los Angeles as Reeve sat back and drank his coffee. They were on Clea's turf now, and the rules had changed. For a while, she'd be giving the orders.

8

CLEA AND REEVE waited in the foyer of the Browning mansion in Denver's exclusive Hilltop section, looking at the octagonal ceiling thirty feet above.

"Cozy, eh?" Reeve observed. "I could dry-dock the *Argosy* in here and still have room for a couple more boats."

"Shh, she'll hear you," Clea whispered. "The butler said she'd be right down."

"Yes, but it'll take ten minutes to descend that marble staircase," Reeve joked just as a figure appeared on the landing above.

Clea watched the tall, slim woman walk down the stairs toward them, a feat that took only a fraction of the time Reeve had suggested, even though she moved slowly with a model's grace. Then Clea stepped forward to meet Adrienne, the woman whose fabulous smile had once graced the cover of fashion magazines and later lit up a television game show.

"Ms. Moore from *Trends?*" Adrienne asked in a small, hesitant voice.

"Yes, I'm Clea Moore." So this was what had become of Adrienne, Clea thought. Now she was being shown off in another way, as the wife of Carl Browning. It was a life-style that obviously agreed with her. Although no longer young, the smile was still in place, and the jewels at her throat added an extra sparkle.

Clea returned the smile and held out her hand, showing no sign of recognition, only a deference that befitted the occasion. "This is my assistant—"

Reeve finished the sentence. "Jake Halstead. Pleased to meet you, Mrs. Browning."

It was Clea's turn to glance at Reeve and his turn to give a silencing look that told Clea there was a good reason for the assumed name.

Oblivious to it all, Adrienne said, "I'm so pleased to have you here," in a voice that proved why she'd never had lines to speak on TV. It was small and high-pitched, not a voice that suggested assurance, although Adrienne seemed entirely comfortable in her role of hostess. "*Trends* is a wonderful magazine. I know so many people whose homes have been profiled in it."

"Yours will show up beautifully, I'm sure. Will this be a good time to get some establishing shots?" she asked, careful to show respect for Mrs. Carl Browning's position.

"Of course," came the reply. "I expected you to, and I've made sure to keep the morning free."

"That's very kind," Clea said. "If you could just give us a quick tour so we can get an overview today and set up the formal shoot later. Jake will make notes on what we'll need."

Reeve, trying to blend into the background without much success, nodded and pulled out his pad.

"There's only one problem," Adrienne said, as Clea stifled a moan, expecting an insurmountable barrier. "We're giving a party tonight so there's an unusual amount of activity with the caterers and my full staff...."

"A party!" Clea caught Reeve's eye, and realized she shouldn't jump in so quickly. *A little more finesse*, he

seemed to be saying, *don't ask for an invitation yet.*
"No, that won't be a problem," she responded sweetly.
"Just so we can still get a glimpse of the whole house."

"Of course," Adrienne responded. "Shall we start the
tour here?" She indicated a formal living room adjoining the foyer.

"Perfect." Camera slung around her neck, Clea followed Adrienne.

The room was dominated by a huge stone fireplace
over which hung a painting that could have been a
Turner; if so, it had cost Browning dearly, Clea realized, and proved that he was a very serious collector,
and not just of pre-Columbian statuary. The room was
furnished in English country antiques, not Clea's taste,
but further proof that Browning spared no expense for
what he wanted.

Clea snapped away, commenting casually out of
Reeve's hearing, "This room just begs for a party. I can
imagine it filled with people having a grand time."

"It is a marvelous house for entertaining," Adrienne
agreed. "Maybe this would be a good time to see the
back living room. It's less formal and the parties usually drift that way."

Adrienne led them down a long, wide hallway, which
opened eventually into a huge space with furniture
grouped in settings that looked cozy in spite of the size
of the room. Reeve found his way across muted Oriental rugs and up three gleaming hardwood steps to an
antique billiard table, where he seemed to linger in fas-
cination.

Clea knew better. There was statuary lining the built-
in walnut shelves, but she saw at a glance that it wasn't
pre-Columbian. Reeve, unsure of his judgment, had to
get a closer look.

Adrienne had crossed the room and opened the French doors onto a tiled patio. There was a gazebo at one end, a bathhouse at the other, and in the middle copper frogs perched on lily pads spouted water into a kidney-shaped pool. Beyond the pool, a bright green lawn sloped toward a vast flower garden.

"It's beautiful," Clea gushed, overdoing it a little, she realized, but genuinely impressed.

"During warm weather, we entertain outside as much as possible," Adrienne remarked as she opened the doors for Clea to line up her shots.

"I wonder," Clea said, as if the thought had just hit her, "if we should feature the party in one section of the *Trends* piece?"

"Why, I hadn't thought of that," Adrienne admitted.

"You know, something like, 'How Denver Entertains—a Special Evening at the Brownings'."

"It would be unusual, but I'm not sure what my husband would think." Adrienne became hesitant.

Clea persisted. "You're absolutely right that it would be very different from the other stories about the homes of your friends."

That was the right tack, Clea realized immediately, and Reeve obviously agreed. "Sounds much more interesting than the usual tour feature."

Adrienne smiled her practiced but undeniably beautiful smile. "Yes, it *will* be a nice party."

"I'm sure," Clea agreed, trying to ignore the slight smirk on Reeve's face.

"I have a marvelous florist," Adrienne continued, "and there'll also be a string quartet."

"How lovely," Clea gushed. "Jake and I could come back early this evening before the guests arrive to shoot the preparations. Readers are fascinated by all that," she added conspiratorially.

"I'm sure they are," Adrienne agreed.

Certain she'd won, Clea flashed her own smile, directed at Reeve. If they were at the party, they'd have the run of the house.

"Let me show you the preparations," Adrienne offered.

Clea and Reeve followed her toward the kitchen, their glances carefully surreptitious.

The spacious room was a bustle of activity as servants prepared for the arrival of the caterers. A florist's truck had driven up to the back entrance, and arrangements were being unloaded.

The arrival of the florist was cause for excitement, and Adrienne was called away to confer with him. Reeve took the opportunity to move closer to Clea.

"How're you doing, Jake?" she whispered.

"I'm not sure. Playing the loyal assistant isn't exactly my bag," he admitted. "But you're certainly fawning nicely."

Clea stifled a smile.

"I don't know how much longer I can carry this off, Clea. When are we going to see his collection?"

Clea shrugged, her gaze never leaving Adrienne, who was locked in conversation with the flamboyant florist.

"I haven't noticed anything that looks remotely like the jade statue," Reeve continued.

Clea agreed. "What we've seen so far is legitimate," she said. "I suspect the jade is upstairs somewhere, hidden away from suspecting eyes."

"Can you get us up there?"

"Just watch."

When Adrienne joined them, Clea brushed her apologies aside. "I can imagine the stress of giving a party like this. You must be extremely well organized."

Although a slight flush of pleasure crossed Adrienne's face, Clea noticed that the woman kept a very tight rein on her emotions. "I try to keep the house running smoothly," she attested.

"That's an interesting angle in itself," Clea said, as if with sudden realization. "Make a note of that, Jake. We can show Mrs. Browning getting ready for the party, putting together a guest list, sending out invitations—"

"Actually, this is a benefit for a concert at the civic center," Adrienne said. "The guest list is prearranged."

"I understand," Clea said knowingly, "but you must have input in the arrangements."

"Of course," Adrienne said.

"I assume you have an office?"

"Upstairs—"

"Perfect. Would it be too much trouble for us to see where you work?" she asked unctuously.

Adrienne was more than agreeable, and Clea was pretty sure she had the upper hand as they set off, climbing the vast stairway to the second floor.

The master bedroom was another huge room filled with antiques, a canopied bed, Oriental rugs and soft ivory draperies lining the windows. Clea was beginning to get a surfeit of studied elegance as she followed along to the bathrooms, his and hers; each with a sunken marble tub, Jacuzzi and skylight open to the heavens.

Lifting her camera as if by rote, she took a few shots of Carl Browning's connecting study. All she could be sure of as she focused through the lens was a definite lack of pre-Columbian art.

From the corner of her eye, she saw Reeve in the doorway shaking his head. He hadn't seen anything, either.

Moving on to what Adrienne called her writing room, Clea tried to show some enthusiasm as she snapped the delicate Queen Anne desk surrounded by curtains and slipcovers in a symphony of peach, pale green and ivory. "This will be marvelous," she assured Adrienne. "We can set up shots of you at work, maybe with a social secretary?" That was a good guess.

"I do have someone who helps me," Adrienne admitted.

It was then Clea noticed that Reeve had drifted off, she hoped, to do some sleuthing on his own while she kept Adrienne busy talking about the noted decorator who'd done the house.

When Reeve materialized in the doorway, he nodded, and Clea felt a surge of relief. It wasn't all for naught.

Adrienne, however, noticed nothing as she instructed Clea on the filing system she'd set up, including menus, notations about each party's theme, and even what she'd worn.

There was still more to see. Reeve followed behind as Clea walked beside Adrienne, listening with slowly dying interest as they traversed the floor, finally retracing their steps and passing an unopened door.

A nod from Reeve prompted Clea to ask with a whimsical grin, keeping her voice light, "Is this a secret room?"

Adrienne laughed, a little nervously, Clea thought. "Not exactly, but it is off limits. My husband's hobby is ancient artifacts, and his special collection is in this room. I don't show it unless he's at home."

Clea wondered if Reeve had actually peeked inside but didn't want to look in his direction for verification.

"Oh, yes," Clea said with understanding, "American Indian artifacts, aren't they?"

"Almost," Adrienne replied. "Actually they're pre-Columbian, from Mexico and South America. How did you hear about his collection?"

Clea thought she'd detected a hint of suspicion in Adrienne's voice, and tried to relax. "Hmm. I'm not sure." She wrinkled her forehead. "Maybe from Bitsy Shruggs in Atlanta, or was it Naomi Fox in Beverly Hills? Do you remember, Jake?" she asked, having successfully mentioned two of the wealthiest and best known hostesses in the country.

Adrienne visibly relaxed. "I don't know Bitsy, but Carl and Naomi's husband are very good friends."

"Everyone's heard of Carl—and Adrienne—Browning," Clea said, overdoing it a little but completely sure of herself now. "I'd love to photograph the famous collection."

"I'm not sure Carl would agree to that. I really must ask. He's wary about showing this collection because of stipulations in the insurance. They're very strict about public displays, you know." Adrienne was already moving down the hall, and there was nothing they could do but follow.

"I can imagine," Reeve interjected as they started down the stairs. He seemed acquiescent enough that Clea suspected he had a plan in mind. Whatever the scenario, they weren't going to see the artifacts yet; that much was clear.

In the foyer, they continued plans for photographing the party, with Adrienne excited, almost to the point of animation, when the front door opened.

Carl Browning's presence silenced her immediately.

He was a small man, in his mid-fifties. His thinning hair was still jet black and flicked back unstylishly, but his clothes were straight out of the fashion pages and he had the physique of a man ten years younger, well muscled and trim, sporting a tan not acquired in the mile-high climes of Colorado.

His presence seemed to make his wife a little anxious, and Clea understood perfectly. Carl Browning possessed the coldest blue eyes she'd ever seen and a demeanor that left no room for pleasantries.

"Carl, darling," Adrienne said in a voice far from confident, "this is Clea Moore from *Trends* magazine and her assistant. They're planning a spread on the house."

Browning looked totally disinterested as he shook hands with them.

Feeling the need to press every advantage, Clea suggested, "I think you may know my father, Charles H. Moore from Los Angeles—"

"We've met," Browning said. "In Saratoga, I believe."

Even though there wasn't the slightest hint of enthusiasm in Browning's voice, at least he'd acknowledged her remark, and Clea felt she had a foot in the door. "Your house will show up beautifully. I'm sure this will be one of our best articles, and when we highlight the party—"

"Photographing our party?" Browning turned his eyes on his wife.

"I thought—maybe—"

"Certainly not, my dear. That isn't a good idea at all."
The words were gentle, but the message was clear. The
party would not be photographed.

"But I've invited Ms. Moore and Mr. Halstead."

"Of course, you should see that their names are
added to the list. Chuck Moore's daughter and her assistant are certainly welcome, but there'll be no photographs. Some of my friends might object, and I want
them to enjoy themselves."

"But it's a benefit, Carl, not really our party."

"My dear, you realize that many of our friends are
on the civic center's board of directors."

"Of course," Adrienne acquiesced.

"We'd be glad to get releases," Reeve attempted.

"No, I don't want them disturbed. No one can have
a good time with cameras recording every move. Now,
you two young people are welcome to attend and enjoy yourselves."

Nodding her thanks, Clea for the first time was at a
loss for words. Her plan didn't seem to be going right
at all.

Reeve came through for her. "We'd planned to use
some party preparations in the article, but it might be
a good idea to focus on that, showing Mrs. Browning
at her desk, interviewing the suppliers, going over the
guest list with a representative from the fund-raising
committee. We could stay over for a day or two and set
everything up after the party."

Clea came back to life. "We could even get some
background on how you choose the right dress by following you on a shopping trip, that kind of thing."

Adrienne looked hopefully at her husband.

He nodded. "That would be fine, but no pictures at
the party. Is that understood?"

"Absolutely," Clea said. "We'll just come and have a good time."

OUTSIDE IN THEIR RENTAL CAR, Reeve gave Clea a look of mock despair. "I don't ever want to be in that position again."

"As my assistant?" she asked with a grin.

"Whatever the title, I was inundated by an overdose of enthusiasm."

"That's not my usual style—but she responded, didn't she?" Clea asked in her own defense.

"*He* is another story. Have you ever seen eyes that cold?"

"And the smile of a shark," Clea added with a shiver.

"Which proves my point, Clea. This is too dangerous for you to mess with. Let me handle it from now on." Reeve had recognized something hard and unscrupulous in Browning that prophesied a dangerous situation.

"Forget the party? Never, Reeve."

He'd expected that.

"At first I thought we'd lost everything when he said we couldn't shoot the party, but this way is even better." Clea almost chortled with glee. "We go tonight, mix with the guests, find the jade and then—"

Reeve stopped for a light and glanced at her sternly. "And then what?"

"Nothing." She looked out the car window.

"I know you, Clea. You think we should take the jade, but I've been against that from the beginning. Besides, there'll be alarms all over the place."

"What?"

"Clea, you've been around these kinds of people all your life. You grew up in this way. Didn't your father have an alarm system?"

"No, actually, he didn't," she said.

"Well, that's unusual for a man as powerful as your father, but then he wasn't a crook."

Clea shot Reeve a quick glance. "In spite of all his other faults."

Reeve smiled. "I didn't say it; you did. Anyway, the place'll be secure."

"Then we'll have to find the alarm, turn it off and go back later—"

"No, Clea, no heroics. Not now; not later."

Clea turned and met Reeve's eyes directly. "You know as well as I do it's the only way, and you're planning something, too. I know it. Why else would you give a fake name?"

"In the first place, taking the jade to Mexico is one way of handling this but not the only way. Secondly, giving a fake name was just instinctive. Street smarts, I suppose. It's all right if Browning checks up on you, but what if he tries to find out about Reeve Holden and learns I skipper a charter boat out of Southern California? That would certainly arouse suspicion, which I don't plan to do; in fact, if it wasn't so difficult to pull off, I'd leave you at the hotel tonight and go to that party alone."

"But you know that would never work," she commented.

Since Reeve had already admitted as much, he didn't need to reply.

"There's only one problem," Clea said.

"I'm glad you're willing to admit at least one."

"We don't have anything to wear."

"Clea, let's be serious—"

"This *is* serious."

"Clothes are hardly our major problem in this little scheme," Reeve said.

"They are if the party's black tie."

"A tuxedo?" He grimaced.

"You can easily rent one," she soothed, but Reeve could see the glint of amusement in her eyes. She was enjoying his discomfort.

"Really?" He was joking now. "I'd hoped to lay down a few hundred dollars to buy one outright."

"You can laugh about it, but I really will have to buy something," Clea said, "something spectacular."

"You've been looking for an excuse."

She made a face at him. "You can drop me off at the nearest department store for a shopping spree. I'll see you back at the hotel in a couple of hours."

Reeve drove to a nearby shopping center. Stopping at a light, he was surprised to see Clea reach for the door handle.

"Wait a minute. I'll turn at the next corner and let you out near the entrance."

"Never mind," Clea said as she opened the door, "Carl Browning's not going to have me run down in broad daylight." With that she got out of the car, blowing Reeve a kiss.

The light turned green, and he had no choice except to go on without her, continuing toward the hotel, scolding Clea to himself. She was taking this much too lightly, as if it were some kind of game. She just didn't realize how dangerous a game it could be. Browning might not have people run down in the street, but if Charlie was right, his methods were rarely less violent.

Reeve pulled the rental car into its slot but didn't get out immediately; instead, he tried to analyze what he'd gotten himself into. The whole situation was getting more out of control by the moment, which wasn't the way Reeve liked to run his life. He usually knew exactly where he was going and what he was doing. Every time he got involved with Clea, he seemed to lose control. He was enough of a realist to know it was happening again.

Finally, Reeve went to his room, still unable to shake the premonition that tonight they'd be walking into the lion's den, and above all he'd need to keep a cool head.

CLEA WAS ON HER WAY to the department store when she noticed a little boutique that looked very French. A dress in the window caught her eye; it wasn't at all the style she'd usually wear, but the occasion called for something different, so she decided to go in and try it on.

"It's very elegant, isn't it?" the saleswoman commented when Clea emerged from the fitting room. The vivid scarlet dress she donned was cut high in the back with poufed sleeves, and had a tight-fitting bodice and tulip skirt that flattered Clea's elegant figure.

"Yet at the same time, it's so—French," the woman added in an accent that was also very French, "and just a little bit naughty."

Clea couldn't help but agree. While everything else was primly covered, the neckline was low and cut in a wide square to revel an expanse of bare skin.

"The French do have a way with clothes," she agreed, intrigued by the dress's dual message. It was provocative and sexy, and at the same time evoked a sense of mystery. Whatever the combination, it worked and

Clea saw no reason not to make the most of her evening at the Brownings'. It was going to be an adventure, and the sense of daring she got from the shockingly scarlet dress felt just right.

"I'll take it," she said without glancing at the price tag, which she knew would be as outrageous as the dress.

"Anything else for *mademoiselle*?"

"Of course," Clea realized, "I'll need shoes. Hope I can find something."

She did. They were black and strappy, and she added a pair of sheer silky stockings.

Before Clea finished dressing, the saleswoman returned with a black silk nightie decorated with strategic bits of lace. "Perhaps? For later?"

Clea shook her head but couldn't resist holding up the nightgown, which was soft as a moonbeam. "I love it, but I really shouldn't—"

"But how sad to go through life only doing what we should. That would be no fun at all." The woman had a delightful accent and a charming smile. "Just let me show you a few of our prettiest things."

"Well—" Clea said, aware that her resistance was fast eroding.

"Yes, I thought so. There is someone, a special man in your life."

"Oh, no—"

"Please, you must not deny. It is difficult to fool a Frenchwoman about romance."

Clea left the store half an hour later with her scarlet dress, shoes, hose, the black nightie and a handful of lacy panties and bras, wondering what in the world had gotten into her.

Standing on the corner waving for a taxi, she real-ized she was acting like a bride on the eve of her wed-ding, buying piles of frothy lingerie. "What am I doing this for?" she wondered aloud.

A cab pulled to a stop at the curb and Clea got in, perfectly aware of the answer. If she hadn't been able to fool the saleswoman about the man in her life, she certainly couldn't fool herself.

REEVE STOOD in front of the mirror in his hotel room, tied his rented black bow tie and stood back to check his appearance. He shrugged. It was the best he could do. He'd been lucky to find a tux that fit him, Reeve thought, smiling ruefully. Once, long ago, it hadn't been so easy. His mind raced back in time, remember-ing.

Charlie and Clea had insisted he come to a formal party at the Moore house, and Charlie had dragged him to a rental store for his tux. It was ill-fitting, and he'd felt uncomfortable the whole night, especially under the elder Moore's cold-eyed scrutiny.

Pulling himself back to the present, Reeve glanced at his watch. "Show time," he said softly and knocked on the door to Clea's room. At her response he stepped in, and his heart caught in his throat.

"Reeve," she said with a smile, "you actually look comfortable."

He managed to return the smile. "I guess you were thinking about the last time," he said, but the words sounded forced, and Reeve knew why. Just the sight of her had taken his voice away.

"Yes, I was."

Her blond hair hung loose and seemed to float around her shoulders, and below there was the rich, golden expanse of her neck and throat, and the rise of her breasts, barely covered by the red dress. Below the hem of the tight-fitting dress, her legs seemed to go on forever. He'd never seen Clea look so sexy and yet so demure. His eyes swept her up and down again, as if he couldn't get enough. "You look beautiful," he whispered.

Reeve could tell she was a little embarrassed by the intensity of his gaze as she turned away, teasing, "Oh, this old thing." She ran her fingers down the fabric of her dress. "Just something I picked up in a bargain basement." Then, totally out of character but so appealing, she struck a pose like one of the models she often photographed, swinging her hair around her shoulders.

The affect on Reeve was colossal, but there was one problem. "Oh, drat," Clea said.

"What's the matter?"

"I think I caught my hair in the hook on this dress. I must not have fastened it properly." She lifted her hands behind her neck and tried to free the thick strand of hair, and the movement almost did Reeve in.

All he could do was stare, for as she raised her arms, Clea's breasts thrust forward, and he could see not only their rounded outline but the little buds of her nipples taut against the fabric. He took a deep breath.

"Let me see if I can extricate you," he offered, "before you rip the dress."

"Oh, would you? This is so tiresome and stupid." If Clea had noticed his nervousness, she didn't let on. In fact, the calmness of her demeanor just made Reeve more anxious.

He stepped behind her and for a long moment enjoyed the sensation of being so close. He could feel the

warmth rising from Clea's body and smell the heady
fragrance of her perfume. Tonight it was more provocative and alluring and seemed to wrap them in its sen-
suous cloud.

She'd pulled up her hair and bent her head forward
to give access to the hook, and the line of her neck was
open to him, soft and smooth and very kissable. He
leaned over, his lips only inches from the enticing col-
umn.

"Reeve?"

"Just deciding how to tackle this," he lied.

"I know, it's absurd, but try not to break the hook.
I'd hate to arrive at the Brownings' party with a safety
pin in my dress."

"Oh, what the heck," he joked. "We can always run
by a bargain basement and pick up another one."

"Reeve—"

"All right, all right. I'll be careful." He'd lightened the
mood but done nothing whatever to lighten his own
feeling. Reaching out, he attempted to concentrate on
the job before him, trying desperately not to touch the
tempting flesh.

"All right, let's have a try," he said. It was impossible. His fingers felt like giant thumbs, incredibly
clumsy, as he fiddled with the hook, trying to unwind
the tangle of her hair.

"How's it coming?" she asked lightly.

"Fine," he mumbled, using all his willpower to concentrate on the fragile operation. His emotions cried out
to slip his arms around her waist and pull her close, to
let his hands slide gently upward to her breasts. He shut
his eyes for a moment, thinking about what it would be
like to kiss her neck then let his lips linger on the softness near her chin.

Clea could feel the heat from Reeve's body, and the warmth of his breath against her neck sent little shivers along her spine. She wondered if he was aware that his closeness was torture to her. She felt her heart racing, her blood turning hot and warming the surface of her skin.

Surely, he must have noticed what was happening to her as his fingers inadvertently caressed the sensitive skin of her neck. He was driving her wild, and in a moment she'd either have to pull away or turn and raise her lips for his kiss.

Then the moment passed.

"There," he said, and she felt a little pull. "Your hair's free, and your dress is intact."

For a long moment the room was quiet, with only the sound of his breath and hers. His fingertips lingered at her neck, and neither of them moved.

Then he stepped away.

Clea brushed her hair back. "Thanks," she said. "Another crisis dealt with." Her eyes were bright and her face flushed. She turned quickly to the mirror, buying time, willing her heart to slow its frantic pace, and trying desperately to keep him from knowing how his closeness had affected her.

"But more to come, I'm sure," he said.

Clea remained turned toward the mirror, unsure of what his words meant.

"We may run into some problems at the Brownings' tonight."

Clea felt a surprising chill of disappointment. "Yes," she answered dryly. "I know."

"Just remember to play it cool, Clea. No chances, okay?"

"I don't want to stir up suspicions any more than you do," she answered, turning to meet his eyes. "We'll pretend to enjoy ourselves, and we'll look for the jade." She flashed him a mischievous smile showing that she remembered his earlier lecture. "Look, don't touch," Clea reminded herself aloud.

It was Reeve's turn to look away. "That's it exactly, Clea," he replied, "advice for both of us. Look, don't touch."

Before she could say anything else, Reeve was at the door. "Come on," he said, "let's get this over with."

9

"WE COULD HIRE A LIMO," Clea suggested as she and Reeve took the glass elevator to the bottom of the huge domed lobby.

"Not a chance," he said, unable to justify such extravagance.

"Reeve, it makes perfect sense."

"We have a rental car," he reminded her.

"All right. If you want to wait in a line around the block for the valet parking—"

They stepped off the elevator and crossed the Brown Palace lobby. "What gives you the idea we'll have to wait in line?" Reeve asked, aware that she probably knew what she was talking about.

"I've been to hundreds of benefits, Reeve. The crowds all arrive fashionably late, and somehow no one ever thinks to keep the lines moving with a bigger staff of valet parkers." She glanced at her watch. "I hate to tell you, but we're already fashionably late. A limo is the answer."

Not about to agree, Reeve suggested, "What do you say to a cab?"

It was the perfect compromise.

THE TRAFFIC BEGAN TO STALL two blocks from the Browning house. Reeve shot Clea a look that said he didn't want to hear *I told you so,* and asked the driver to stop. "We'll walk," he explained as he opened the door and helped Clea out.

"You know all the answers," he admitted.

"This has been my career," Clea said, not terribly proud of the fact.

"And your life," he added. Defensive, Clea glanced at him quickly, before realizing that the remark hadn't been meant to hurt. Besides, it was true. This was how she'd grown up.

The party was in full swing as they headed up the circular drive to the Brownings' house, pausing to announce their names to a security guard at the entrance.

"What did I tell you?" Reeve whispered as they were passed along. "The place'll be fortified."

"Tonight, only," Clea retorted.

Reeve shook his head in amazement. "Persistence will get you nowhere," he concluded.

"Let's not make any rash decisions," she said, as they climbed the stairs and were swept up into the party.

Several hundred of the famous and near-famous, the rich and about-to-be rich mingled in the foyer, and Reeve played a game with himself to determine which was which.

Knowing where the real party was from their earlier visit, Clea led Reeve to the back of the house. There the low roar of conversation was occasionally pierced by a shrill burst of laughter and the sound of music floating into the house from poolside.

They found the host and hostess, made their obligatory acknowledgments and stationed themselves by the French doors, playing the social game.

Reeve knew Clea had been right to head for the heart of the party first. Later, they would return to the foyer and wait for the moment to ascend the staircase. The jade was upstairs, but they had all night to find it.

Returning from the bar, Reeve found himself momentarily alone, nursing his drink and holding on to Clea's. He saw her across the room talking with an attractive older couple who'd waved her over. Apparently she knew quite a few people at the party, and that didn't surprise him. This was her milieu; she was as much at home as he was uncomfortable here.

As she moved toward him, Reeve thought once again how beautiful—and sexy—she looked. In a room filled with women dressed by the world's best designers, Clea still looked special. He noted with a jolt of real jealousy the predatory looks some of the men gave her as she walked past. It was getting tougher and tougher for Reeve to come to terms with the fact that she wasn't his and never would be.

But tonight no one else knew that. He could pretend. Not a man given to fancy, he nevertheless managed to fantasize. He watched her approach, stop to smile at an acquaintance before moving on to him, taking the glass from his hand which she touched briefly in the exchange, then turn her smile on him. They were a couple in that moment, and it felt damned good.

It was all he could do to keep from leaning over and kissing her, just to show all those envious eyes whose woman she really was. But he restrained himself.

"Hi." She smiled at him, seemingly oblivious to his thoughts. "Any action?"

"All's quiet so far. Who're your friends?" He couldn't keep the touch of envy from his voice.

"They're from L.A. Friends of my parents."

"Of course," Reeve said dryly.

"They want me to photograph their daughter's coming-out party." A slight grimace accompanied her words.

"You don't look very enthusiastic about it."

"She's a nice girl, and Lord knows I've shot enough deb parties to do it in my sleep."

"But?"

She smiled. "But it's wearing a little thin. I'd like to use the time to try something different."

"Like what?" he prodded.

Clea was vague. "I'm not sure exactly, maybe something like I wanted to do years ago when I was a kid." Clea paused for a moment then reminded him, "But this isn't the time to contemplate my future. We have other more pressing business."

"Can't deny that," he said. "Do you think we should make our move now?"

They looked around the room. Most of the guests were involved in conversation with one another or concentrating on the plates of hors d'oeuvres being passed by the hired catering staff. "This is as good a time as any," she responded.

"Remember," Reeve said, "if anyone asks, we're just scouting photo possibilities for the layout."

They headed through the house to the foyer where a large crowd of latecomers gathered. Threading their way through, they slipped up the stairs. It was an easy move and not an obtrusive one since other couples had gathered on the stairway to avoid the crush of bodies.

The sound of laughter and conversation followed until they were alone in the long hall. Silently, their footsteps muffled by the thick pile carpet, they headed for Browning's collection room. Reeve reached for the doorknob, which turned easily in his hand.

He looked around, saw no one, and taking Clea's hand ducked inside.

"No security," Clea commented.

"Which means the place is probably wired."

"With alarms?" Clea asked, startled.

"Clea, we're talking a major collection here—I think."

They looked around at what could have passed as just another anteroom with comfortable furniture, deep shelves and low lighting. But on second glance they could see that it was much more.

The shelves were lined with fragments of carved stone stelae covered in Mayan hieroglyphics. There were rows of terra-cotta figurines, human and animal, fantastical and realistic. The small jade pieces displayed in glass cases constituted the focus of the collection. Gleaming exquisitely under the soft, hidden lights, they ranged in color from shades of palest green to bright turquoise.

Reeve took a step forward. "Be ready to run if we set off an alarm."

Clea held her breath, waiting. Reeve took another step. They heard only the muted sounds from the party below.

"I bet he's planning to show off his treasures tonight," Clea whispered as she reached out to touch one of the cases.

Reeve's low warning stopped her. "Don't forget the alarms, Clea."

She withdrew her hand but not her gaze. The treasures were extraordinary. "What I wouldn't give for my camera now."

"Yeah," Reeve said. "One of those mini spy—" He broke off in midsentence. "Someone's coming." Voices could be heard ascending the stairs.

Clea's eyes swept the room. "There's a closet—"

"It's the best we can do," Reeve said as he slid back the louvered doors with one hand and grabbed Clea's arm with the other, pulling her into the small enclosure.

The closet, used as a storeroom, held filing cabinets and built-in storage shelves lined with neatly labeled boxes, leaving very little room for Clea and Reeve.

Their bodies by necessity were thrust close together, and instinctively, whether for protection or compactness, their arms encircled each other's waists. Clea's face was pressed against Reeve's shoulder, breasts against his chest, pelvis angled onto his hips.

There they stood, hardly daring to breathe, hearts pounding in unison as Browning and his companion entered the room.

"When are you going to sell me some of this collection, Carl? It looks to me like you're getting greedy."

"You know it's not for sale, Al. But I do have a new piece you might be interested in. Let me cut the alarm."

Clea drew her breath sharply. Reeve had been right; there was an alarm. She'd pulled her hand away from the glass case just in time.

Unable to see into the room, she stood straining, listening for a clue to the alarm system. First there was a scraping sound, then a pause followed by a click.

The unknown Al let out a low whistle of approval.

"A beautiful piece of jade. Olmec, if I'm not mistaken." He sounded very sure of himself, and Clea had no doubt what he was looking at. It was Charlie's jaguar.

"Exactly," Carl answered, "and obtained at no small sacrifice, I might add."

Clea started at that remark. Her brother was without a doubt the sacrifice in question.

Reeve held her firmly as if telegraphing the need for her to remain absolutely calm and quiet. She obliged, even relaxing a little in his arms.

In spite of the closeness of danger, the possibility of discovery, Clea found herself intensely aware of Reeve. How could it be otherwise when his body was molded so tightly to hers? She could feel the steady movement of his chest, and Clea was certain she heard the slow beating of his heart as a counterpoint to her own, racing rapidly.

As the men continued to examine the jade, talking in low voices filled with admiration, Reeve held Clea more tightly as if to protect her in some way. Her arms snaked around his waist until it seemed as though they truly were one. She was infused by the heat from his body, an all-pervading warmth that was making it very difficult for her to concentrate on what was happening just a few feet away.

Somehow the danger of their situation only heightened the exquisite awareness of being in Reeve's arms. Because it was becoming almost impossible for her to deal with, Clea shut her eyes and forced herself to listen to the voices.

"The piece is museum quality," Browning was saying, "but I rely on your discretion as usual in letting that be our own special secret."

The man called Al gave a low laugh. "We've had a few special secrets over the years, haven't we? No, I'll keep this one if you won't mention that Roman bronze in my garden that everyone thinks is a marvelous copy."

"No problem. We fellow collectors need to protect each other." There was conspiratorial laughter and once again Clea heard the sliding noise and the click of a switch as the alarm was reset.

Then there was the opening and closing of the door and, finally, silence.

Clea raised her head to look at Reeve, whispering very softly, "I think they've gone."

Reeve didn't answer right away but stood stone-still, his body molded against hers. "Be patient for another minute or two. Just to be sure he's not coming back."

Clea nodded, her eyes still on his face, which was shadowy in the faint light that filtered through the louvered doors. His lips were inches from hers, and she wondered momentarily if he was going to kiss her. She knew such a thought had no place in a situation like this, but she couldn't control it.

Kissing Clea was very much on Reeve's mind. In fact, it had been since the moment they were thrust into the closet, their bodies pressed so intimately together. He was painfully aware of her, every curve and hollow molded lovingly to him.

Somehow Reeve had withstood the temptation to take her into his arms in the hotel room. He smiled to himself at the futile warning they'd shared—look, don't touch. It had taken less than an hour for him to break that rule. He was touching her now, and he'd never wanted anyone as much in his life.

How was he going to get her back to the hotel without holding her again? And even more importantly how was he going to stay out of her room? A few more minutes of her body so beguilingly pressed to his and he'd lose what semblance of restraint he possessed. He'd begin kissing her and never want to stop.

Before that happened, Reeve forced himself to take a deep breath and reach for the closet door.

He opened it quietly and looked out. "Coast clear."

They slipped out, still staying close, but it was suddenly obvious that Clea had something else on her mind. "The jaguar's here, Reeve," she reminded him, looking toward the cases on the far wall.

"No, Clea." He didn't even want her to see it.

"We could take it, Reeve," she insisted. "Didn't you see where the alarm was?"

"No," he replied. "I could see a section of the room through those louvers, but Browning moved out of view when he cut the alarm. It doesn't matter, though. We're not taking anything; we're getting out of here. Now." He reached for her arm.

Clea moved away. "We can't leave, not when we're so close to the proof."

"Oh, yes, we can." Reeve caught her in his grasp this time and didn't let go as he pulled her from the room.

Just as they stepped into the hall, they heard voices coming up the stairs again. "Damn," Reeve said under his breath. "Here comes the second tour."

They hurried across the hall where Reeve opened the first available door and pulled Clea in. This time she didn't resist. Reeve knew what he was doing, and all she could think about was what could have happened if he'd let her go through with her desire to steal the jade.

They were in a dark room where they stood motionless as Browning and his guest, this time a woman, passed by. As soon as they heard the door to Browning's collection room open and close, they went out, down the stairs and into the foyer.

Clea grabbed a glass of champagne from a passing waiter and downed it. Then she looked at Reeve.

"Thanks for saving us," she said. "It was a narrow escape. Now can we get out of here?"

"No farewell to our hostess?" he asked with a grin.

"She won't notice."

"We'll need to call a taxi," he said, relaxed now and enjoying the fact that Clea had finally decided not to take any more chances.

"There'll be cabs cruising on the major streets."

"We may have to walk a while to find one," he said, still grinning.

"That's okay with me."

Once outside in the cool night air, something happened to Clea. They hadn't walked more than a block when she began to feel exhilarated. The momentary fear she'd experienced, followed by a desire to be out of the Brownings' for good, was replaced by something else.

It was a sense of accomplishment and adventure, and it manifested itself in physical changes. Her cheeks flushed, the blood seeming to sing in her veins, turning her skin hot and then suddenly cold. They'd done it, she thought. They'd located the jade jaguar. Now it was time for the next step.

Reeve moved purposefully toward the main street, where he began looking for a taxi, with no success. "You probably have to call taxis in this town," he commented.

Clea lagged behind then rushed ahead, not caring if they had to walk all the way to the hotel. "What a fantastic night," she chortled, finding her voice at last. "And no one has a clue what we're up to!"

Reeve walked on, ignoring her.

"Now all we have to do is go back tomorrow, find the alarm—"

Reeve stopped then, turning on her with an expression that mixed anger and frustration. "No, Clea. Enough is enough. I got you out of that house safely, and now I'm getting you out of town. Tomorrow you're getting on a plane to L.A., and I'm going to Mexico and report to Charlie. That's it. No more adventure, no more danger. I've had it."

Clea wasn't ready to back down. "We're so close. We're almost there. Just another day or two and—"

Reeve's hand grasped her shoulders. "No, Clea, we're leaving. Both of us. It's over." He wanted to shake some sense into her, to remind her that they'd been two novices thrust into a dangerous game for which they didn't even know the rules. It had gone on far too long, and the half-detective, half-thief facade he'd tried to maintain for her was in danger of cracking.

Clea's eyes were shining with anger. "Is that what you want? Just to walk away?" There was desperation in her voice, and Reeve knew that she was no longer talking about Charlie and the jade; she was talking about them. "Answer me, Reeve. Answer me! Do you want it to be over?"

Her eyes met his and locked in a look that was honest and direct. Reeve knew he couldn't walk away from it.

"No, dammit. That isn't what I want. *This* is what I want." In a white-hot flash of passion that possessed him totally, Reeve pulled her close, and his mouth found hers.

Clea clung to him with a wild and primitive need that fed her desire. Reeve felt drawn downward into a great vortex of passion from which there was no escape. It was just as he'd imagined. Once he touched her, once he kissed her, there'd be no turning back.

It was all Reeve could do to keep himself from throwing her into the bushes and making love to her then and there, but he managed to remain upright and let Clea work her magic on him.

Her mouth tasted like wine sweetened with honey, and her tongue met his in a questing exploration as their breaths mixed and mingled.

All around the nighttime sounds of the street faded away, and there were only the two of them, alone in another world.

Then a car approached at breakneck speed, brakes squealing as it took the corner next to them. The noise brought Reeve back to the here and now, and he relaxed his hold, one arm still around her, as they walked toward the intersection where by some stroke of luck a taxi had stopped at the light.

Clea didn't really remember getting in the taxi. It seemed as if their kiss had never ended. Her hands entwined in Reeve's hair, pulling his face to hers, responding to his kisses with a passion that seemed to lift her out of herself, her body trembling as she strained toward him with a desire as powerful as his own.

When he moved his hand from her waist to her hip, down the shimmering material of her dress, stopping on her leg, caressing her through the silky stockings, Clea realized what could happen next. She also realized they were in the back seat of a taxi driving through the streets of downtown Denver.

"Reeve . . ."

"I know," he said, and she felt the words more than she heard them. They were warm, damp against her mouth. "This could get out of hand." Then he chuckled softly. "It *is* out of hand, but we'll be at the hotel soon."

"Not soon enough," Clea whispered.

"I guess we're not angry at each other any more," he said, his hands still moving provocatively along her leg.

"I guess not," she answered shakily.

"I wonder what the driver in that car thought?"

"What car?" Clea asked as she moved her hands down his chest.

"You really didn't hear the brakes squeal?"

Clea shook her head. "I was mesmerized."

"I still am." Reeve nibbled on her earlobe. Talking helped. The fire inside had died down enough to get him to the hotel, but he knew that what happened after that would set them both ablaze.

"But I do wonder what the cabdriver thinks," Clea whispered.

"Let's don't ask," Reeve replied as they pulled up in front of the Brown Palace Hotel and the driver looked at them over his shoulder with a wide grin.

Reeve shoved some bills, probably far too many, into the extended hand, and they tried to look casual as they went into the hotel, but Reeve couldn't resist whispering in her ear, "I've wanted to make love to you from the minute I saw you upstairs in that red dress. I wanted to throw you on the bed and say, 'To hell with Charlie and the Brownings.'"

"You can still say it," Clea reminded him.

"To hell with them both," Reeve exclaimed, eliciting a raised eyebrow from the desk clerk as they passed, and a giggle from Clea.

They stopped to kiss once more before stepping into the crowded elevator. Even there, surrounded by other guests, Reeve was unable to keep his hands off Clea. He had to touch her back, her cheek, put one finger on her lips, which were already swollen from his kisses.

It was a surreal ride to their floor with indistinct faces and blurred voices. Then the door slid open and they stepped into an empty corridor.

"I think it's the first time we've been alone tonight," Reeve said, taking advantage of it by sweeping Clea into his arms and carrying her to his room. Along the way she lost a shoe, but neither of them noticed the ebony patch left behind on the carpet.

Somehow they made it down the hall and into Reeve's room. It was dark, and he almost stumbled as he crossed the threshold and searched for the light switch. The bright flash was momentarily blinding, and Clea reached up to shield her eyes.

"Wait," Reeve said huskily. "Close your eyes." He crossed to the bed, put her down, and touched her once gently on the forehead before going to turn out the light.

"No," he said as if to himself. "That's not good. I want to see you."

He reached over and turned the bedside lamp on low. It cast a warm glow across Clea's reclining body and brought an audible sigh to Reeve's lips. "So beautiful," he whispered, bending over, his hands working swiftly and surely to somehow slip the red dress down and off, revealing the wisps of lingerie beneath.

The touch of his hands, which had been nearly frantic in the taxi, was gentle now, relaxed, as he slowly unsnapped her stocking from the lacy garter belt. "Such an improvement over panty hose," he said. "You know how to drive me crazy, don't you?"

He tenderly rolled her silky stockings down, one at a time, over her slender legs, then removed the garter belt and tossed it aside. His easy motions became a little more hurried as he hooked his thumbs under her panties and pulled them down over her hips.

Clea lifted her buttocks slightly and in an instant another garment dropped to the floor, but Reeve was still touching her, moving his hands from her ankles up her calves and thighs to her abdomen, lovingly, warming her skin with his fingertips.

Just when Clea began to wish that his caresses would go on forever, he moved away. Her eyes, which had been half closed in delight, opened just in time to see him smile.

"I think it's time for me to do some disrobing," he said almost casually, only the catch in his voice evidencing his feelings as he struggled out of his clothes.

Then, naked, he leaned down and kissed her on all the places his hands had caressed. "This is much better than the back seat of a cab," he murmured.

Clea looked up at him and smiled, drinking in the strong lines of his body, the broad shoulders and chest, well-muscled arms and legs. "Or a storage closet," she said shakily.

She reached out for him, and her hand grazed the hard evidence of his desire.

Reeve gave a sigh of pleasure and took her in his arms, and Clea felt suddenly at home, where she belonged. She ran her fingers along the line of his chin, nuzzled close as he took her fingers in his mouth and tenderly sucked each one. She kissed his shoulder, tasting his salty skin, and remembered how close they'd been in that cramped closet less than an hour before, hampered by the two men on the other side of the louvered door. "At least we don't have to worry about Carl and Al now," she said.

"Nope. It's just you and me. Not even any clothes to keep us apart," he replied as he moved his hands to her breasts, where he unhooked the last impediment to their lovemaking and tossed the flimsy bra on the pile of clothes beside the bed.

"And no talk of jade to keep us from doing . . ." She kissed his shoulder, tasting his salty skin, "This."

"Jade?" he asked. "What jade?" He let his lips tease a line along her neck to the hollow between her breasts, now exposed so beautifully to him in the golden light. He caressed them while his thumbs rubbed her nipples until they peaked and tightened under his touch.

Clea moaned in pleasure and let herself give in to the exquisite tension inside her that had been building all through the night, growing stronger and stronger.

"You like that, do you?" he asked teasingly as she squirmed beneath him. "Then you'll like this, too." His lips found her nipple, and he used his tongue to tantalize until Clea thought she could bear no more. All the long night, she'd waited for this and now it was happening, but with agonizing slowness that both excited and frustrated her. She ached for more.

"Reeve . . ." Her hands played along his back, feeling the delineation of each hard muscle, warm and moist now with the heat of their passion. She dug her fingers into the taut skin, pulling him closer.

He buried his head against her breasts then moved downward, searching with his lips for another warm place to kiss and nibble. He lingered on her softly rounded stomach, moistened it with his tongue, then moved his lips along the line of her hipbone.

Clea quivered beneath him, holding on to his shoulders and, as he moved lower, burying her hands in his thick hair. She caught her breath when he kissed the inside of her thigh and cried out when at last his mouth discovered the most intimate part of her.

Lying back, releasing her hold on him, Clea let the sensations he was causing wash over her in waves of pleasure. But it wasn't enough. She wanted something more for them both.

"Make love to me, Reeve," she murmured.

"Now and for the rest of the night," was his promise as slowly he raised up and over her, sliding into her welcoming softness. He moved deliberately, watching the play of emotions on her face, the longing, the need, the satisfaction.

Then his own desire caught fire from hers; not the near-primitive lovemaking they'd experienced before, but a slow, sure exploration of their passion.

She responded to him just as she had all those years before with a rhythm that matched his own. It had been perfect then; it was more than perfect now. His movements became stronger, faster, keeping time with the pounding of his heart and the blood thrumming wildly in his veins.

Clea raised her hips to meet him, calling out his name, and her voice was a beacon to him. He answered with the only words he could find. "I love you, Clea."

"And I love you, Reeve. I'll never love another man."

"I'll love you forever, till the day I die."

When Clea opened her eyes and looked into his at last, Reeve knew that this was the most intimate moment of his life. Not only were their bodies joined but somehow their souls had touched tonight.

He kept holding her, and she clung to him as if not wanting to end the wonder they'd shared. He could feel with every fiber of his being all he'd seen when he looked so deeply into her heart and soul.

Kissing her softly he could only say, "I won't forget, Clea. I'll never forget this."

"Nor will I, Reeve," she answered, smiling and curling up close to him, her pliant body pressed against his. And wrapped in the glow of their love, they slept.

10

REEVE'S ARM was around her waist, holding her near. His shoulder was a comforting pillow for her head. It was bliss just being beside him, her body warm against his. His voice murmured her name. . . .

Clea remembered the dream; it was the same one she'd had their first night in Denver, and she'd awakened from it to find herself alone.

This time she struggled to maintain the dream, but the bonds of sleep began to fall away as daylight insinuated itself beneath her eyelids. She clamped them closed, trying to bring it all back.

It was no use. The dream was over.

She opened her eyes, staring at the ornate ceiling, remembering. Maybe, just maybe, it wasn't a dream, she thought as she tentatively moved her hand along the sheet.

This time her hand met with solid flesh. She moved it upward slowly to be sure that what she felt was real. She explored the hard sinews, the taut skin, the relaxed muscles and knew there was nothing imaginary about what she touched. Reeve was there beside her.

Slowly Clea opened her eyes. The early morning sun that crept in the room filled it with a kind of golden glow. The light spun a halo around Reeve's dark hair and glistened on his skin. Her hand remained where it was, feeling Reeve's chest rise and fall with each deep, easy breath.

She couldn't take her eyes off him but lay there silently, enraptured by the peacefulness that enveloped them. This was better than any dream, Clea thought, for she had the leisure to examine Reeve thoroughly.

The youthfulness she'd long remembered was replaced with a more mature but no less handsome look that had hardened his chin, strengthened his jawline, added lines along each side of his mouth, between his brows and at the corners of his eyes. His skin was much darker after years of exposure to the sun, and there were slight flecks of gray in his hair just at the temples.

She liked this new Reeve much better than the boyish one but, she had to admit, he was no less stubborn and determined, no less proud. None of that had changed.

With a half smile playing on her lips, Clea inched forward until her mouth was next to Reeve's. Gently, almost teasingly, she began to kiss him into wakefulness, nibbling on his chin, tasting his lips with her tongue, kissing first the corner of his mouth, then his bottom lip, lingering but very lightly so as not to waken him. Yet she wanted nothing more than to have him awake beside her again just like last night.

It had been so perfect, and she was still wrapped in a luxurious haze of sensuality, heightened by coming out of her dream to find that he was really there.

He lay quietly, lost in a deep sleep. Or so it seemed. But she could detect the flicker of an eyelid and feel the quickening of his breath.

"Faker," she whispered. "I believe you're actually awake."

His answer was to wrap his arms tightly around her, pulling her body against his. He kissed her long and unhurriedly, taking his time, enjoying the moment to its fullest.

"What a great day," he finally murmured, his face hidden beneath the bright tangle of her hair.

"How do you know? You haven't opened your eyes."

Reeve opened one eye then closed it against the sunlight. "I know it's a great day," he said sleepily, "because I woke up with you beside me." He pulled her even closer, snuggling comfortably. "Now that I have you here, I don't think I'll let you go. Let's call room service and spend the rest of the day in bed."

Clea sighed and hugged him mightily. "I feel the same way. I guess Charlie was right. This little venture did get us back together."

"Charlie," Reeve echoed with a groan as he finally opened his eyes. "I suppose someday we'll need to get back to Santa Inez and tell him what we've learned."

"At least you're saying 'we' now," Clea observed.

Reeve took her hand, entwining her fingers with his. "We're a good team, partner. I can't deny that." He raised her hand to his lips.

"We are that," Clea seconded. "Good partners."

They were both silent for a moment, and Clea wondered if Reeve's thoughts were running in a pattern parallel to hers—partners and lovers now, but what about tomorrow? What about the next day and the next, after Mexico and Charlie; would they be together then?

She wanted to talk about the future, and yet she was afraid, remembering that night in Santa Inez. They'd talked the next day and it'd been awful. She couldn't bear to go through that again. Of course, it might be different this time, Clea told herself, but she didn't want to take the chance. In the dark, in the heat of passion, they'd murmured words of love, but to repeat those words in the light of day was a leap of faith that she wasn't ready to take.

There *was* something they could discuss, though, and she broached the subject with far less trepidation than talk of commitments would have caused. "We still have one more job, partner."

Reeve pushed himself up against the headboard, a frown cutting across his forehead. "I'd ask what you mean, but I'm afraid I already know."

"We have to go back to the Brownings," she said, forestalling his objections by plunging ahead. "There are two very logical reasons. First, if we don't, they might become suspicious, check up on us. They might even hide the jade. If it goes into a bank vault, we'll never get near it again."

Reeve didn't comment so Clea felt her way clear to go on. "Besides, we have no solid evidence, no proof, no photographs of what we saw. We owe Charlie that much, and all we have to do is get back in the room."

"You're right. We do need proof. If we go back on the pretext of shooting the magazine story, it shouldn't be that difficult to take a photograph of the jade."

"Yes, that's a thought," she said, "but—"

"I'm not sure I like that 'but.'"

"What we really need is the jade," Clea blurted out, turning away from Reeve as she adjusted the pillow so he couldn't read what was written on her face. It was hope, but it was fragile. He'd gone along with her more than once during this trip, and in order for him to do it again, Reeve himself would have to make the decision.

"That's not part of the master plan," he reminded her.

"But it could work," she said, adding tentatively, "I've been thinking . . ."

Reeve groaned. "That always gets us into trouble."

She tried to ignore his remark, hoping that he would see her point. "Browning can't have us arrested even if we take the jaguar, because it's stolen, and he'd have to admit that to the authorities."

Reeve raised his eyebrow and tried to give her a stern look. "You sound like your brother. Maybe larceny runs in the family."

"You know I'm right." Clea tried to sound sure of herself, but she was aware that everything hinged on what Reeve thought about the plan. If he nixed it, then she would have to give it up. She sensed that convincing him against his will wasn't going to work again.

"Let's look at this logically, Clea," he said, and she breathed a sigh of hope. At least he was considering the possibility of taking the jade.

"He could send his thugs after us; that's what happened to Charlie. I don't want it to happen to you. Or me," he added with a grin.

"Charlie wasn't smart. We are. If we get out of town before Browning knows it's gone, cross the border into Mexico and put the jade in the museum . . ."

"Wait a minute," Reeve interrupted. "This is beginning to sound like something worthy of James Bond. We're not exactly in that league."

Clea put her hand out and touched Reeve's arm. She knew that he was thinking about the idea because he wasn't objecting as much as usual. Her only hope was that his mind could have been working over the same plan. She chanced it. "You've been thinking about this, too, haven't you?" she asked softly.

"You read minds now?" he quipped.

"Tell me the truth, Reeve," she prodded, sure she was right. She had to be right.

Reluctantly, he answered. "Yes, I've thought of taking the jade, clearing the whole thing up once and for all. But," he warned before she could get too excited, "if we do it, we'll need a plan, a good one. No more winging it, Clea."

Clea pushed a strand of hair behind her ear. Her eyes were serious now that she realized Reeve was in this with her. They could succeed!

"Okay, let's plan," she said. "We get in the house under the guise of photographing Mrs. Browning at home. Somehow we lose her and get into the collection room." Then she had a prophetic thought. "The door could be locked."

"It's only a latch, not a dead bolt. I checked. I can trip it with a credit card," Reeve said. "Browning depends mainly on the alarm."

"Which we need to find." Clea was getting excited now. "At least we know what part of the room it's in."

As they planned, Clea became more sure that they could succeed. Lying in bed with Reeve's arm around her shoulder, his mind working in conjunction with hers, it all seemed wonderfully simple and perfectly right. Except Reeve kept bringing up problems.

"We'll have to have a replacement for the jaguar."

"I don't think we'll find Olmec jade in Denver," she said, "or anything resembling it that we could afford." She was suddenly feeling despondent.

"I know, but we can at least pick up a piece of green jade, glass even, to fill the space. Browning will notice eventually, but it might buy us some time. I imagine there're plenty of curio shops in Denver. That can be my job," he decided. "I'll find something that'll pass for the jaguar while you rent the photographic equipment."

"No problem. I can pick up a few things to make us look professional and legitimate."

There was a long pause as they realized the plan could work. Excitement quickly gave way to a sort of lethargy in both of them. "I guess we need to get started," she said finally, not wanting to leave the warm intimacy of their bed.

Reeve agreed as he stirred slightly and with a glance at the clock prepared to get up. "Wait a minute," he said, one foot on the floor. "It's barely after eight." The foot slid back under the cover. "Nothing will open until nine. That gives us plenty of time to . . ."

Clea felt her heart quicken. She was sinking under his spell, even though she knew that what was happening between them was still transitory. Some time they should talk about it—about last night and what it meant to them, for them. But not now. Her need for him was too strong; there was no room for discussing anything more. Not yet; not now.

Boldly she met his eyes. "Time for what, I wonder?"

Reeve grinned and pulled the sheet away from her naked body. She could feel her skin grow hot under his hungry gaze. Slowly, he reached out to touch her, running his fingers along her cheek to the corner of her mouth.

Clea's lips opened, and she bit gently on his fingertips.

Reeve laughed a low, teasing laugh, and continued his exploration, running his now damp fingers along her neck to the hard line of her collarbone then to the hollow between her breasts.

Clea held her breath, eyes closed. She felt the amber sunlight pour over her, adding its warmth to the heat Reeve had generated. His hand caressed the roundness of her breast. She could feel her nipples grow taut and hard. Deep inside dwelt a need that only Reeve could satisfy, and she raised her eyes to his, asking him with her look to meet that need.

The desire she felt was mirrored in his eyes, and Clea let go of her breath contentedly as the sweet remembered flow of passion swept over her, washing away everything but the moment and the touch of his hand.

Eyes still locked, reliving fantasies, promising unknown delights, they wrapped themselves in each other's arms to capture the passion that was theirs alone.

Clea had the sudden feeling that if they didn't grab the moment, it would be lost to them.

The thought frightened her at first, but not for long. Desire took the place of fear and brought back the longing. She gave herself gladly to it.

"I'D SAY WE LOOK professional enough." Reeve tried not to buckle under the weight of the bags he lugged, filled with lights, extension cords, stands, umbrellas and additional paraphernalia he couldn't even identify.

"I want to be impressive," Clea said, following along with cameras slung around her neck and extra lenses in her camera bag.

"And to that end you rented every piece of photographic equipment in Denver?"

"Just so you'd look like you knew what you were doing," Clea teased as she pressed the Brownings' doorbell.

"Why, good morning, John," she said, greeting the butler amiably when the door opened almost immediately. "We're here to set up for the shoot today."

The butler's face was impassive and not at all welcoming.

"For the magazine photo story," Clea said, pressing on, relentless.

Still no acknowledgement from John.

"We were here yesterday," Clea reminded him. "I'm Clea Moore, and this is my assistant . . ." She paused, reaching frantically for Reeve's assumed name, but it didn't matter in the slightest to John.

"Yes, ma'am. I recall," he said, without budging.

"Well, we arranged to return today and take the pictures."

"Mr. Browning has gone to the office, and Mrs. Browning will be at her health spa this morning. Neither of them left instructions about two—um, photographers," he said, clearly unimpressed.

When Clea started to waiver, Reeve stepped in. Boldly, he shouldered past her and John, stepped into the hall and deposited his equipment on the marble floor.

"That's okay," he said calmly. "We have instructions from Mrs. Browning herself. I believe we're supposed to start upstairs in her writing room, just like she showed us yesterday, right, Clea?"

"Uh, right, right," Clea said, following his lead. Elegance wouldn't work here; no one could top John in that department, so apparently they were going with the pushy approach. She could only hope he would consider them so far beneath him as to be of no consequence.

"Then let's get on with it," Reeve said, heading for the stairs.

"One moment, please," John demanded.

Clea felt her knees grow weak. This wasn't going to work! Getting to the jade with Adrienne around would have been difficult; with John it was going to be impossible.

Beyond the foyer Clea could see a crew busy at work cleaning up from the night before; she imagined John's job was to keep a careful eye on them. She doubted if it was one he enjoyed. If only they could tempt him away.

Reeve had the answer. "Didn't Mrs. Browning want to show some of the staff in the interior shots?" he asked Clea.

She stepped in quickly. "Of course. Who do you suggest, John?"

"Most of these people are outsiders, not household staff at all," he said.

"We wouldn't want them anyway," Reeve said. "We'd want the person in charge. That would be you, wouldn't it, John?"

"Of course, but I couldn't possibly—"

Clea tried to control her excitement. Reeve had found the answer—the butler was vain!

It didn't take long to talk him into leading them upstairs to the writing room, protesting all the while, but not, Clea noticed, very vehemently.

Guided by Clea's instructions, Reeve began arranging the lights. She'd decided to do it right, which would serve a twofold purpose. John would be taken in by the professionalism but because of the time involved would also become impatient.

It worked. After setting up, taking several light readings and making adjustments of a few inches here and there, she could see John begin to squirm.

"Not very glamorous, is it?" she asked, not looking up from the viewfinder.

"I didn't realize it would take so long," was John's response as he gazed over his shoulder, expecting some catastrophe from the floor below where he should have been watching over the cleanup crew.

"Just a few minutes more," she assured him as she took another reading.

"Clea is a perfectionist," Reeve said between clenched teeth. Obviously, her delaying tactics were getting to him, too, but Clea didn't know what else to do. If only John would just give up and leave. But he stood by, stoically.

She could feel little rivulets of perspiration running down her back, between her shoulder blades. For all she knew Adrienne could return from the spa at any moment. That would be a problem but nothing compared to her husband's arrival on the scene, which was also a definite possibility. They needed to get the jade and get out, but John wasn't cooperating.

Finally, Clea couldn't stall any more. "We're ready," she said, directing the butler to his place and beginning to click away, assuring him that the expression was just right. "We're getting a perfect view of the room, and your presence really adds to the shot," she assured, wondering what the hell she was going to do next.

Then fate intervened in the form of a very loud crash from downstairs. It had the sound of shattering crystal, and it was music to Clea's ears.

Before she could look up, John was halfway out the door. "I'll have to find out what is happening," he said.

"Sure, go ahead," Reeve responded airily. "We'll still be setting up the next shot when you get back."

"We'll call you," Clea added. She certainly didn't want him rushing back.

Standing by the door, Reeve watched until John disappeared down the stairs. Then he turned to Clea. "Are you ready for this?"

"I'm ready to get out of here," Clea said, "but only after we have the jade. Come on."

Silently, they moved into the hall. With Clea acting as a lookout, Reeve fumbled with the latch to Browning's room. "Got it," he said after what seemed like an eternity.

As they stepped inside Clea realized that her heart was pounding at an alarming rate. She wiped her sweaty palms on her shirt. "Let's find that alarm," she said, trying to keep a steady voice. "We heard a creaking, sliding kind of noise. So it's under something or behind something—"

"Or *in* something," Reeve added as he began moving around the room. He worked slowly, deliberately, his demeanor in contrast with Clea's building anxiety.

A minute passed, then another. She slid a painting aside, fumbled with cabinet doors, looked behind books, wondering how long they had before John solved his problems downstairs.

Her breath seemed to be coming in gasps while Reeve was quiet and calm, moving carefully from one area to another in the quadrant of the room where they'd determined the alarm was located.

Another minute passed, and Clea began to wonder why she'd gotten involved in this. It was her fault, because she'd been the insistent one. Now she was beginning to think Reeve's caution was well founded.

At that moment, her hand touched a carved wooden chest on a lower shelf. When she tried to push it aside she realized that it was somehow attached. She opened the top.

The creaking, sliding sound alerted Reeve. "Got it?"

"Yes," she breathed, flicking with switch concealed inside.

"Get your camera then. We don't have much time."

"Oh, really?" she asked, her nervousness turning to irritation.

Reeve shot her a look as he opened the case where the jaguar was displayed.

It was beautiful. There was no doubt about that, but Clea didn't stop to admire the statue. She set the camera on automatic and began shooting, not worrying about setting the stops. There wasn't time. They'd been in the room at least five minutes, and that was four too many. After half a dozen shots from different angles of the jade and other artifacts, she shouldered the camera. "I'm done."

Reeve removed the jaguar, checking carefully for the marks that Charlie had described before, substituting the imitation he'd bought a few hours earlier. Then he closed the case, switched the alarm on and headed for the door. "It sounds quiet out there." He looked at Clea. Her face was drained of all color. "We've made it," he said. "Just a few more steps."

Clea nodded, wondering if she could take those steps. Reeve opened the door, and they slipped into the hall.

From downstairs came the noisy clatter of the cleaning team. Covered by that sound, they moved to Adrienne's writing room where Clea sank down on a convenient chair, her head in her hands.

"You were wrong about the Moore genes," she said weakly. "I'm not cut out for a career of larceny. That was the most awful experience of my life, and I think

I'm going to be sick." Her head felt light; her stomach was turning cartwheels.

Reeve rested his hand on her shoulder comfortingly. "You did fine, Clea. You found the alarm, we have the photographs—and the jade. Now all we need to do is get out of the house."

"Now," Clea said. "I want to leave right now."

"That would cause suspicion," Reeve warned. "We should stick it out."

Clea shook her head. Horrible visions were writhing before her eyes. Adrienne could return home and cause a scene, maybe even call her husband—or the police. Worse, she could expect a photo session. Then they'd be trapped for hours in the house, during which time Carl Browning would return, check his collection and realize at once what had happened.

Clea knew that her fears were unrealistic and that panic was taking over, but she didn't care. She wanted out, and she wanted out now. When she heard footsteps coming down the hall, she breathed a heavy sigh. That was the last straw; she couldn't take any more.

John appeared at the door. "Hired cleaning crews are not to be depended—" He broke off after a glance at Clea. "Miss Moore, are you all right?" he asked.

"She's not feeling well," Reeve replied.

"Too much partying last night," Clea said weakly.

"You do look quite pale, Miss Moore. I'll have the maid bring a cold cloth for you."

Clea protested, but John headed for the stairway where he called out to someone below and had his request filled in no time.

Reeve took the cloth and placed it on the back of Clea's neck. With her head down, eyes shielded, she was able to hide her reaction to John's next words.

"Mrs. Browning called on the private line down-stairs, and when I told her you were here, she said she'd be right home. She seemed very agreeable to your plans for the morning." John sounded smug, as if he'd made the correct move in letting them into the house.

Clea groaned, and Reeve knew what she was thinking. There would be hours ahead of filming Adrienne at work and play while the jade burned a whole in his pocket and the possibility of Carl returning unexpectedly hung over them. There was only one alternative, and unknowingly Clea had set it up.

"That's too bad, John, because we're going to have to leave. Miss Moore is not in the condition to finish shooting. She needs to get some rest, possibly even see a doctor."

All Clea had to do was lift her stricken face for John to agree. Still, he didn't give in immediately. "Mrs. Browning will be disappointed."

"No more than we," Reeve lied as he began packing up the equipment.

Clea made an effort to help, but both men fore-stalled it. "Just sit still," Reeve advised. "I'll have everything ready in a minute."

It was more like fifteen minutes before he managed to get the equipment packed and, with John's help, loaded into the van they'd rented.

As the minutes crept by, Clea found it more and more difficult to control her impatience. Adrienne could ar-rive at any moment, causing them to go through the whole litany of lies again. But she might not be as eas-ily fooled as John.

Clea threw a desperate glance at the two men. To her anxious eyes, they were moving in slow motion. They'd refused to let her help, and all she could do was stand by and mentally wring her hands while gazing surreptitiously down the driveway, praying that Adrienne was stuck in traffic somewhere.

Finally the men were finished, the door of the van shut with Reeve and Clea inside. She waved her thanks to the butler, telling Reeve under her breath, "Hurry, please. I can't take one more minute of this."

Reeve turned out of the circular driveway and started down the street just as a silver Rolls-Royce approached. "It's Adrienne," he announced. "I'd say our timing was right on the edge."

Clea leaned back against the seat and gave a tremendous sigh of relief. "Sorry to fall apart like that, but I've never stolen anything before. Even if what I stole was already stolen—twice," she explained.

Reeve laughed. "You don't have to apologize to me, Clea. But I tried to tell you it wouldn't be easy."

"I know, and I won't doubt your good advice again," she promised.

"Actually, we were well served by your conscience attack."

"I think it was just nerves," Clea admitted.

"Whatever, it got us out of there, but I'm afraid it may also cause some problems."

"Problems? Great. Just what we need."

"I imagine Adrienne will try to reach you later."

"She doesn't even know where we are staying."

"Clea, think about it. The Brown Palace is the first place she'll try. That's my fault. I should have gotten us rooms somewhere else."

"It doesn't matter. We've checked out anyway."

"Yes, with the photo shoot unfinished. It looks pretty suspicious."

Clea moaned. "What if she tells Carl?"

"I'd say we can count on that," Reeve replied.

"Then he'll start wondering about us."

"And notice the jade is missing," Reeve added reluctantly.

"We'd better head for the airport as soon as we drop off the photo equipment."

Reeve disagreed. "We could be hours getting out of here, and he's bound to check the flights. He doesn't know my name, but he knows yours."

"I don't have to use it," Clea suggested.

"Of course not, but I imagine Browning has ways of finding out what he wants to know. We'll be easy to track to Santa Inez. He might even have a welcoming party waiting for us."

"Reeve—" Clea was clearly panicking.

"Calm down," he cautioned. "We have other options." He pulled up to the rental store where they'd gotten the photographic equipment and turned off the engine. "The next stop is to get gas and a map. While Carl's concentrating on the airports, we can backtrack, drive a few hundred miles to an unlikely airport, fly into Dallas or Fort Worth and change there for Mexico. Not Santa Inez, though."

"Reeve, why not?"

"That's our obvious destination. It's where the jade came from, where his thugs got to Charlie. We'll have to sneak in by a back door. Agreed?"

Clea nodded with a sigh. "I'm sorry," she said.

"Sorry?"

"About this mess. I was the one who insisted we take the jade, and now both of us are on the run. It's like a bad movie, Reeve." She was joking, but her voice sounded disconsolate.

Reeve managed to laugh at the joke and ignore the despair. "I'm a grown man, Clea. I knew what I was getting myself into. Besides, if I hadn't joined forces with you, you'd have tried this on your own."

"And ended up in jail—where Charlie'll be soon." She sighed again. "If he's not there already. At least this has taught me a lesson," she continued. "From now on, I'm going to think things through, take time, look at all the ramifications. I've made mistakes, and to keep me out of worse trouble, you've gone along. No more snap decisions and spur of the moment actions," she decided.

Starting to unload the equipment, Reeve paused and cut his eyes toward Clea. The color had returned to her face, but she hadn't yet recaptured her spirit of adventure. "Does this mean we don't share a room tonight?" he asked.

Clea put her hand on his leg. "No, it doesn't mean that at all. I've been thinking about going to bed with you ever since I got *out* of bed with you—if that makes sense," she added.

"It makes perfect sense." Reeve squeezed her hand. The danger they'd faced at the Brownings' had left him keyed up, almost buoyant; in fact, it was going to take a while to wind down, and he was glad for the extra time their detour would give him.

Reeve hadn't told Clea any of the things that were on his mind. He needed the right moment to find the words that would express his feelings. They were words that needed to be said, but they would have to be chosen very, very carefully.

11

IT WAS LATE AFTERNOON when they spotted the airstrip on the outskirts of Double Springs, Colorado. Reeve stopped the van, and they got out. He headed toward the low cinder-block building while Clea walked around, stretching her legs. They'd been driving all day, and they were still in Colorado; and Clea was tired.

After a glance at the map in Denver, they'd realized driving west over the Continental Divide was out of the question so the most sensible course was to head east across the plains toward Kansas. Somewhere along the way they'd find a town with a feeder airline that could get them close enough to make connections to Mexico.

Even if this little strip was the answer, they were still only on the first leg of a long trip. But Clea wasn't concerned. They were together in the venture, and as tired as she felt, she was also exhilarated just being with Reeve. Their adventure had certainly taken on another dimension, and in spite of the danger, she'd never felt happier.

She watched Reeve as he came toward her. He looked relaxed, not tired, not even concerned about the predicament they were in. He also looked dusty, a little sweaty, and very handsome.

"We're in luck," he told her. "There're two flights a day into Wichita. Seems as though the cattlemen around here need to get to the big city now and then."

"Great," Clea said. "Not that I don't love the plains of Colorado, but—"

"You're getting a little tired of driving through them?"

Clea nodded. "When can we get a flight?"

"Well, that's the catch. We missed the afternoon flight by an hour." He didn't give Clea time to moan. "But we have tickets for nine o'clock in the morning. Until then, let's see what Double Springs has to offer."

It was a typical cattle town, or what Clea had always imagined such a town would be like. The air was heavy with dust and heat, and the main street was lined with seed and hardware stores and saloons—old-fashioned buildings with latticework facades.

"It looks like a movie set," Clea said. "If only there were horses instead of pickup trucks."

"It's the modern version of a Hollywood western," Reeve decided. "There's even the requisite hound." He pointed to a dog sleeping peacefully in the middle of the sidewalk, oblivious to the traffic around him.

"Let's stay at that hotel," Clea said, pointing out the most decorative building, Etta Turner's Hotel and Saloon.

Reeve eyed the clapboard structure laced with gingerbread curlicues suspiciously. "The ticket agent at the airport recommended a motel on the outskirts of town."

"Obviously he was unaware of our sense of adventure," Clea said.

Reeve hedged.

"Motels are so ordinary, Reeve. Miss Etta's has character and charm and—"

"Lumpy mattresses," Reeve added, "but I'm game." He swung the van into a parking place. "Just don't egg me into a fight with the cowboys," he warned. "I've had enough excitement for the day."

"There probably isn't a cowboy in this town," Clea said airily. "This is the modern version, remember? Ranchers use helicopters and computers nowadays."

Only later did she learn how wrong she was.

THE HOTEL TURNED OUT much better than Reeve expected. Their room was simply furnished with a white iron bed and pine tables and bureaus, but it was clean and bright. Throw rugs adorned the wooden floor, and the flowered wallpaper gave the room a homey feeling. Clea sank onto the bed, which wasn't lumpy at all.

"Now if there's plenty of hot water, we're in heaven."

"You go first," he said. "But don't be extravagant."

"In and out in five minutes," she promised and was almost true to her word.

While Reeve showered, washing away the day's dust and grime, he was overcome by all sorts of fantasies—Clea standing beside the bed as the towel she'd been wrapped in dropped to the floor, Clea stretched out on the bed with only a sheet covering her nakedness, waiting for him, Clea reaching out to take him in her arms.

He dried off quickly and pushed open the bathroom door. "Clea—"

The bedroom was empty except for their luggage. Reeve quickly checked his shaving kit where the jade was still safely hidden. Then he looked for Clea's camera. It was gone.

Reeve wasn't alarmed because he knew exactly where the camera was. It was strung around Clea's neck as she roamed the town, doing what came naturally, taking pictures while there was still time in the waning sunlight.

He thought of going after her then decided against it; this was Clea's time to do her own thing. He'd wait.

By the time Reeve finished shaving and dressing and had located another hiding place for the jade, Clea breezed into the room.

"This town is fantastic," she exclaimed. "There's even a livery stable. I mean a real one, where an old man was shoeing horses. I think he's an Indian," she threw in parenthetically. "I got some great shots."

"Hi, I'm glad to see you."

"Oh, Reeve. I'm glad to see you, too." She gave him a kiss on the cheek. "I didn't think you'd mind if I took off for a little while." Clea put her camera in the case then took it out again and slung it around her neck. "You never can tell what we might see."

"You're right there. Double Springs is a tourist's dream."

Clea laughed. "Well, not exactly, but it's filled with cowboys, which was a real surprise. They've come in from the ranches for Friday night. All ages, all sizes— real cowboys, Reeve."

"I'll take your word for it."

"Not necessary. You'll see for yourself; besides I have the proof here." She waved her camera victoriously. "Oh, while I was out, I mailed the film I took at the Brownings to my mother."

"Your mother?" Reeve couldn't figure that one out.

"Browning might check my house or my agent or even *Trends* magazine, but I doubt if he'd confront Mother. What kind of story could he possibly tell her? Anyway, I wrote a note asking her to put the film in a safe place and not mention it to anyone."

Reeve nodded. "Good thinking, Clea." Reeve thought briefly about the patrician but formidable Mrs. Moore. No, Browning would definitely steer clear.

Clea was getting an extra roll of film from her camera bag, trying to keep her voice calm and easy, not looking at Reeve as she spoke. "I just thought that Browning or his thugs might come looking for us, and if we didn't have the film, we wouldn't be able to give it to them. Would we?" She turned and looked at Reeve expectantly.

"No, we wouldn't," he said, hating the idea that she might be in danger and yet at the same time admiring her foresight. "That was a smart move, Clea. I should have thought of it."

She got off the bed and sashayed over to him. "That's why I'm here, Reeve, darling," she drawled, "to come up with the bright ideas."

Reeve made a grab for her and successfully pinned her in his arms. She felt so good against him, so warm and alive and full of vitality. Just holding her made his heart beat faster. He buried his face in her fresh, clean hair, inhaling the sweet scent, aware of how much he wanted her, how much he'd always wanted her.

Clea looked at him as if reading his mind. "Let's have dinner first," she said. "I'm starved."

Reeve realized that she had every reason to be hungry; they hadn't eaten all day. "You're right," he agreed, "we'll have dinner *first*." He emphasized the last word with a sexy smile.

But Clea was off on another tangent about Miss Etta's. "I hear the food is great. There really is a Miss Etta, and she makes incredible biscuits. I think I'll try to get some shots."

"Clea . . ."

"Yes, Reeve?" There was a twinkle in her eyes; she knew what he was thinking.

"After the photographs, the incredible biscuits and the great dinner, we have a date—" he pointed to the bed "—right here."

Clea laughed at him, her eyes still sparkling. "Indeed we do, and I have a special treat planned for you."

"And just what might that be?" he asked.

"You'll have to wait and see," Clea teased. "Now come on." She grabbed his hand. "The cowboys are waiting."

Hand in hand they descended the wide stairs to the lobby. From below came the sound of music and laughter. Saturday night in Double Springs was heating up.

"I'll meet you in the restaurant in ten minutes," Clea said. "I want to try and get those shots of Miss Etta."

"For the next issue of *Trends*," Reeve joked.

"No," Clea said, stopping and looking at Reeve seriously. "I'm thinking of something a little more important." She frowned slightly, and her eyes became very thoughtful. "This trip has given me a whole new lease on my career, Reeve. I'm full of ideas and plans."

"I'm glad, Clea." What else could he say? He *was* glad for her, but he was worried about her, too.

Clea missed the extra beat and the silence that followed. She was already heading down the hall, calling over her shoulder, "Order me a nice cold beer."

"No problem," he answered.

Reeve walked into the saloon, found a table and ordered the beer. For a long time, he'd been very sure about his feelings, but he hadn't been able to express them because he still wasn't sure about Clea's. This trip had changed her life. They'd found each other again, but more than that, she'd found a desire to work at something worthwhile, the kind of work she'd backed off from years ago.

Reeve hoped she could fulfill that desire, but he knew it would be difficult, not because Clea lacked initiative but because life had been so easy for her. She could fall into the same pattern again, picking up her life in L.A. where she'd left off, and all that they'd known, all that they'd shared these past days—she could disappear again, just like before.

Reeve brushed the thought aside. This time there'd be a different script; this time it would work.

"SO HOW'S ABOUT an early night, cowboy? I reckon we gotta hit the trail before daybreak tomorrow."

Reeve rolled his eyes heavenward over Clea's attempted western accent. "This place has gotten to you."

"I like it," she said. "I like the steaks, I like Miss Etta's biscuits, I like the beer . . ."

"And how about the two fights we've seen?"

"Well, at least there were no broken bones," she replied.

"And the music?"

"I'm getting very fond of country," Clea decided.

"And the dancing?"

"We'll get the hang of it," she said. "Won't we?"

Reeve laughed. "I doubt it."

"It's been fun, though," Clea said. "And it'll make a great feature."

"It doesn't exactly seem like your thing, Clea."

She reached for his beer and took a swig. "I told you before that I'm changing, Reeve, and I'm much more adaptable than you think. You're stuck with an image of me from the past—Miss Patrician Princess. I'm more than that," she challenged.

"Maybe," he admitted.

"You think I'm one-dimensional?" she asked, sensitive to his feelings about her life-style, her past, all the things that had created the chasm between them years before.

"Not at all," Reeve protested, hoping that she was right and he was wrong. "But adapting isn't always easy, Clea."

"I've done just fine here," she protested. "I'm more comfortable in this setting than you were at the Brownings'."

"Granted," he said, "but we're not stealing anything now."

She took his hand and said, "Except time."

Reeve held on tightly. "I'm glad we have that."

Their eyes met and held as the sounds of the room seemed to fade away leaving just the two of them in a world of their own.

Reeve raised her hand to his lips. "Your getting on that plane with me in Santa Inez was the second best thing that's ever happened to me."

Clea let the words sink in before she reacted. "Second best!"

"Yep, second best." He nibbled her palm then let his tongue caress the pulse spot in her wrist. Clea felt little shivers travel along her spine as a warming glow flushed her skin. "The best thing that ever happened to me was the first time I laid eyes on you ten long years ago." His gaze met hers and held.

Clea felt her eyes fill with tears of joy. "Oh, Reeve, you make me so happy."

He moved his lips to the line of her throat. "Come upstairs with me, and I'll show you just how happy I can make both of us."

Clea knew banjos were still strumming and a few couples were twirling to the lonesome, down-home beat. That was happening somewhere, but it wasn't in her world, in the world she was sharing with Reeve. She put her hands on either side of his face and boldly kissed his lips. "I thought tonight I was going to show *you* something special."

Reeve was already on his feet, tossing bills on the table to pay the check and taking Clea's hand. "I'd almost forgotten," he said. "Can't believe I've been sitting here talking when you had a surprise waiting for me upstairs." He led her quickly from the room.

Together they climbed the stairs, Clea thinking ahead to what she'd planned, and Reeve anticipating whatever it might be.

They opened the door and fell into each other's arms, clinging together. Reeve's hand searched for the buttons to her blouse, but Clea stopped him.

"Tonight I seduce you," she murmured, disentangling herself from Reeve's arms and disappearing into the bathroom to slip off her clothes. She was trembling with delight as she lifted the gossamer soft black gown over her head. It settled along her body like the touch of a lover's hand, revealing more than it concealed with its scalloped lace pattern interspersed with tiny satin bows.

Clea ran a brush through her hair and took one more look at her reflection. She'd never done anything like this before, never deliberately set out to seduce a man. But this was different because the man was Reeve, and more than anything she wanted to give him pleasure.

The thought of his eyes moving over her, his hands reaching for her, was almost more than Clea could bear. She knew the pleasure she would give would be given back with equal intensity.

Taking a deep breath, Clea opened the door.

The shaft of light glided across the floor and illuminated Reeve as he sat on the edge of the bed, his shirt unbuttoned, his tanned skin gleaming. Silently, she walked toward him until the light disappeared and her shadow fell across his body.

He stood up, his eyes burning into her. "So this is the surprise," he said in a voice that was so husky with desire she could barely understand. "It's beautiful. You're beautiful." Reeve reached out and touched the shimmering material. Beneath it, she trembled.

Reeve smiled and enclosed her waist with his hands, gathering the gown between his fingers, rubbing it up and down against her skin.

"You didn't see everything I bought in Denver."

"I'm glad you held something back, but this better be the last one," he said with sexy grin. "My heart couldn't take much more."

"This is the pièce de résistance," Clea replied huskily as she slipped into his arms, kissing his neck, letting her tongue glide along his cheek into the hollow of his ear. She could feel the shiver of excitement that ran through him just as her mouth found his in a long, long kiss.

With a low moan, Reeve pulled away and reached for the buckle of his belt.

"No, let me." Clea's hands were clumsy at first as she fumbled with the belt, finally unbuckled it and pulled it from the loops. "I've never done this before," she said.

"Done what?" Reeve asked. "Unbuckled a belt?"

"No. Seduced a man."

"Well, you're doing fine," he said.

The words barely got out because Clea had tossed the belt away, unzipped his pants and was doing just what she'd meant to do, holding him in a way that she'd never held anyone before, more intimately, more lovingly. Her hands were working magic, and Reeve's raspy breathing was evidence that he was in her spell completely.

But he was still partially dressed. Clea stopped long enough to help him struggle out of his pants and pull off his shirt. Then her hands began their wandering again, playing across his chest first, touching his hardened nipples, moving down the firm line of his abdomen to where they'd been before.

This time Clea felt her breath catch as she tried to speak and couldn't find the words. Reeve dropped to the bed, and holding him around the waist, she slipped down to the floor and settled between his legs. Emboldened, she moved her lips toward the place her hands caressed, and they surrounded the hard shaft of his desire.

She explored him slowly and gently at first, touching and tasting as she felt him grow under her erotic ministrations. As she caressed him, Clea felt her own desire flare like a white-hot flame that was unquenchable in its power.

Reeve buried his hands in her hair. She could feel them pressing against her temples in response to what she was doing to him.

"Clea," he called out, "not yet, Clea," he said huskily. "I want to make love to you."

Clea could tell from his anguished voice that it was time for her to pull away. But there was more to come, more sensual adventure to fill their night.

"When you said you were going to seduce me, you meant it," Reeve told her. "Now it's my turn." His arms went around Clea and pulled her down on top of him as he moved his hands along the length of her body from back to buttocks.

"It's a beautiful gown," he said, grabbing a handful and pulling it over her head. "But there's something more beautiful beneath it."

Reeve rolled over until Clea was beneath him on the bed.

Then she felt him fill her with his warmth and strength. At first it was enough to be there beneath him, to be part of him, but soon the pressure began to build, the need began to devour her until she was moving with him, slowly at first then with an accelerated rush, furiously.

As they crossed the edge of their desire, Clea tried to call out his name, but the words caught in her throat. She closed her eyes, and there was nothing but Reeve and the spiraling explosions of pleasure that took her out of herself and made her one with him.

From far away she heard Reeve calling her name. She came back to him as if in a dream until he was holding her so tightly there was no way of knowing where she ended and he began.

Bodies damp with spent passion, they snuggled together, arms entwined, legs interlocked, breath and heartbeat in perfect synchronization. Reeve locked his fingers in hers and brought her hand to his lips.

There was so much to say, so much that had remained unsaid. He knew he should wait until the passion subsided, but he couldn't.

His voice seemed to belong to someone else. It was so low, so husky. But it was his, and the question he asked was one that had been with him for a long time. "This isn't going to end here, is it?"

Clea raised her head and looked at him. "I was afraid so because you kept saying how it wouldn't work."

"I was wrong," he said.

"I'm so glad." She kissed him again and again. "Oh, Reeve, it *is* going to work. It's going to be so good." She dropped one last kiss on his shoulder and settled in next to him. "I love you so. Reeve—"

"Yes, Clea?"

"I'll never love another man," she said, repeating the words first spoken so many years before.

"I'll love you until the day I die," Reeve whispered in reply as he gathered her close so that there was no part of him that wasn't touching her. It all seemed so real and so right. He smiled into the darkness. There would be a new ending to the script; they were writing it now.

The rest, the lovemaking, the peacefulness of being close together and in love was a comfort to them; one they were going to need because the next twenty-four hours would not be easy.

THEY OVERSLEPT and barely made their flight, and at times Clea wished they hadn't made it at all. She wasn't used to small commuter airlines, and she spent most of the trip to Wichita clutching the armrests, hoping she wouldn't be sick.

From then on the day seemed to go downhill. There was barely time to make the connection in Wichita, and they had to grab their bags and jog through the terminal, arriving at the gate panting and out of breath.

They made it to Texas in a blinding rainstorm, and Reeve joined a long line of disgruntled passengers waiting to buy tickets.

More than an hour later, he returned to the restaurant where Clea was languishing over a very bad cup of coffee. He had two tickets for Ensenada.

Clea looked at them then at him. "Reeve, that's a two-hour drive from Santa Inez."

He sank into a chair beside her. "We wouldn't want a direct flight even if there was one—which there wasn't," he added. "Browning is bound to have the airport watched around the clock."

So they boarded the plane to Ensenada, and just before they landed, Clea's real fears began to take hold.

"What if the customs officer finds the jade?" she asked Reeve.

He reached for her hand, his fingers reassuring against her wrist. "Mexican customs officers never look for anything coming *in*. Just play it cool and relax."

She thought about the statue hidden in the toe of Reeve's tennis shoe. He'd insisted on putting the shoe and its mate in his carry-on luggage, but in retrospect the hiding place seemed far too obvious and slightly ridiculous.

Clea's nervousness increased as they approached the customs area at the Ensenada airport. She glanced at Reeve. He was cool and collected, even cheerful, while Clea felt sure anxiety and guilt were written all over her face.

Her nervousness only increased when they stood face to face with the customs officer. In the past their documents had been given a cursory and disinterested glance. Not this time. The officer reached for Reeve's passport and tourist card, which he studied carefully.

Clea felt perspiration bead on her forehead, and even though she knew it was ridiculous, she began to imagine the worst—their luggage would be searched, and they'd have to explain why they were smuggling in an Olmec. Since there was no logical explanation, they'd be taken to "headquarters," wherever that was, and from there to jail. She wondered how the jails in Ensenada compared with Santa Inez.

A stream of Spanish invaded her thoughts. The agent was talking to Reeve, who looked to her for translation. After a moment of panic while she tried to concentrate, Clea understood and rattled off an answer.

"*El señor gusta Mexico. Mucho.* Me, too. I mean, *me gusta Mexico tambien. Mucho.*"

The words tripped off her tongue in her haste, and Clea was rewarded with a smile at her rapid if ungrammatical Spanish.

Afterward, they were waved through the customs area.

"What in the world was that all about?" Reeve asked, pocketing his passport.

"He noticed that this was your second trip into the country within a week so I told him we loved Mexico. Very much. And right now I do love it," she said, feeling almost home free as they headed for the car rental counter.

"It's not over yet, Clea. We still have a long drive to Santa Inez."

"I know," she answered, "but Browning can't possibly watch every automobile on the road and he won't have any idea where we're coming from. Colorado to Kansas to Texas to Ensenada and finally Santa Inez— it's not exactly a direct route."

Reeve laughed. "And to complicate matters even more for Browning, I think we'll rent a Cadillac."

THEY MADE THE TRIP to Santa Inez in style without even looking over their shoulders. But once they reached the town, Reeve didn't dare go near the hospital, stopping instead to call from a pay telephone.

"Señor Carlos Moore," Reeve requested, handing the phone to Clea. "You take it from here in case it gets complicated."

It did. After being transferred several times, she finally was connected to the nurse in Charlie's wing.

"*Señor Carlos no esta aqui,*" the nun told Clea.

Holding a hand over the mouthpiece, Clea repeated the news to Reeve. Charlie had left the hospital.

"*Donde esta Señor Carlos, por favor?*" Clea asked, hoping they would find Charlie soon.

There was a long silence, then the answer, "Colden fleas."

"Colden fleas?" Clea repeated.

Then Reeve began to laugh. "Golden Fleece," he told Clea, "as in Jason—"

"Oh," she said as Charlie's roundabout message finally sank in. "Jason and the Argonauts. The *Argosy!*"

"Exactly," Reeve agreed.

Clea thanked the nun and hung up.

"Leave it to Charlie," Reeve told Clea, taking her arm as they headed toward the car for the drive to the docks and Reeve's boat.

THE *ARGOSY* BOBBED QUIETLY at rest, basking in rays of moonlight. Clea and Reeve climbed aboard and, moving as quietly as possible, crossed the deck and went below.

Reeve slowly opened the door to the main cabin where they watched without surprise as Charlie swiveled around in his chair to face them. There was a beer in his hand and a big grin on his handsome face.

"Welcome aboard, kids, and at the risk of repeating myself, what the hell took you so long?"

12

"EXTRAORDINARY, most extraordinary." Luis Valdez, director of the museum in Santa Inez, spoke almost reverently in his slightly accented English. "To think that we have our jaguar back." He looked at Charlie across his antique desk. "You are a man of honor, Señor Moore."

Reeve caught Clea's eye and then looked away. Honorable was hardly the label for Charlie even though his behavior during the past eighteen hours had been exemplary and very unnatural. With little urging, Charlie had agreed to return the jade statue to the museum, make a clean breast of the whole situation and take whatever consequences followed.

So far, Reeve noted, the punishment didn't seem to fit the crime. Somehow Charlie was turning into a hero.

Señor Valdez went on, "Our joy at having this fine piece back is very great. We never thought to see it again. We will contact the police immediately with the hope of tracking down our former employee who took this from the museum."

Reeve could see Charlie's Adam's apple bob nervously. "I guess...you'll be calling the police about me, too," he said.

At that point, Clea couldn't keep still. "You realize, señor, that my brother really didn't have anything to do with the actual theft. He—"

Reeve reached over and put his hand on Clea's arm. The look she flashed him showed she understood his message. The time for interfering in Charlie's life had passed. She sealed her lips and settled back in her chair.

"I didn't know it was stolen at first," Charlie explained, "but as soon as I saw it, well, I guess it was obvious."

Silently, Valdez nodded.

"I was wrong to get involved, *señor*. I have no excuse."

"But you have made amends," Valdez said, "and I see that you already have received punishment of a sort." Charlie's cast and bandages made his punishment obvious.

Charlie nodded, and Reeve realized they were all holding their breaths, waiting for the director's pronouncement.

"So," Valdez said, "as director of the museum, I choose not to press charges. You are free to go, Señor Moore."

Charlie jumped to his feet, grabbed Valdez's hand and pumped vigorously, hugged Clea and slapped Reeve on the back. "I owe it all to you two. You really came through for me."

Valdez sat back and rang for his secretary. "And now that the business is taken care of, will you have coffee with me?"

"Of course," Clea said, relief evident in her voice. "A little celebration seems in order."

"*Café, por favor,*" Valdez told the young woman who appeared at the door.

"What will happen to Browning?" Charlie asked as he settled down. "Will he be apprehended?"

"I can assure you of that," Valdez said. "As soon as the *señorita* sends us her photographs of the artifacts in his collection, we can begin to identify them. They will be recognized throughout the art world, and proper authorities will be contacted. Sometimes the wheels of justice grind slowly, but Browning *will* be punished, thanks to you, Señor Moore."

Clea couldn't hold back her smile as she saw Reeve raise his eyes to the heavens.

AN HOUR LATER they stepped into the bright sunlight of Santa Inez. "I really have to hand it to you, Charlie. You lead a charmed life," Reeve said.

"I feel as though I've been given a second chance," Charlie responded. "And I'm sure as hell not going to blow it this time."

"A new Charlie?" Clea teased, but she felt hopeful.

"Brand new." Charlie's voice was serious. "I've really heard what Reeve's been saying about my life. This little episode has done a lot to teach me responsibility." Charlie laughed. "Maybe at last, Charlie Moore, aged thirty-two, is going to grow up." He shook Reeve's hand. "All I can say is thanks. I owe you, pal."

"Oh, no," Reeve said. "That's all over. No more debts, Charlie. We're calling it even now."

"That's a deal," Charlie said, laughing and swinging Clea off her feet. "You're the greatest, Sis."

Clea was laughing, too. "Now that it's all over and the ending is happy, I have to admit that it was fun." She linked her arm in her brother's. "Let's keep the celebration flowing. How about lunch?"

"Not for me," Charlie said. "I'm picking up my luggage and heading to the airport for the first flight back to the States. Valdez is a nice guy, but he might change his mind. I'm going home."

"For once, your brother is right, Clea."

"I think this man wants to be alone with you," Charlie told his sister.

Clea kissed Charlie's cheek. "I hope so because I certainly want to be alone with him. See you in L.A., big brother."

CLEA SIGHED with contentment and looked out over the shining waters of the Pacific. The sun was setting, filling the sky with pink and purple streaks that were reflected in the blackening sea. She and Reeve walked hand in hand through the narrow coastal streets of Santa Inez.

They'd had a long, leisurely dinner and were threading their way to the hotel, in no rush. The adventure was over, and everything was winding down. It was very peaceful.

They stopped and kissed, slowly, easily. It all felt so right. Clea held on to Reeve and sighed deeply. When they'd met again ten years after the first time, Clea had thought that whatever happened in their adventure for Charlie would be over for them when the quest ended. But it wasn't over. It was just beginning.

The street opened into a tiny square, green and enticing. There was a wooden bench by an old fountain where they sat down just as dusk fell. They were completely alone, and the night seemed to belong to them.

When she looked at Reeve, Clea had a moment of anxiety. He seemed less peaceful than she'd expected, lost in deep thought, the lines of his forehead furrowed. His were eyes fixed on some point on the distant horizon.

"This is wonderful, isn't it?" she asked hesitantly.

"The very best," Reeve responded, and Clea's anxiety passed.

"It'll be even better when we get to California. I've been thinking about all the things we can do together.

I want you to meet my friends, and Mother and Dad will want us to spend a weekend, I'm sure, and—"

Reeve interrupted in a voice that was quietly thoughtful. "Sounds as though you've been doing some planning."

She had. How could she help thinking of their future when it was the most important thing in her life?

Once again, Clea glanced at Reeve, but it was dark now and she couldn't read his expression. Her voice was tentative when she asked, "You do want to see me when we get back, don't you, Reeve?"

He looked at her then. It was a direct look, intense and almost desperate. Even in the darkness, it made Clea's heart constrict inside her chest.

"I don't think we should go back." He got up and walked over to the fountain.

Clea could feel the tension, but still she didn't understand. "Not go back?" she repeated.

Reeve turned toward her. At that moment the moonlight filled the square, and they could see each other clearly.

"We will be together, won't we, Reeve?"

Reeve didn't answer immediately. This wasn't going the way he'd planned. He'd wanted to be more romantic, more subtle, but when she'd started to talk about home, her parents, her friends, he'd been overcome by a premonition: if they went back, what was between them would begin to fall apart.

"I think there's something we should do first," he said.

"What is it, Reeve?" She was leaning toward him, confusion written on her face.

Reeve knew it was all wrong to throw it at her this way, but he had to know how she felt, where she stood. What he was going to say was risky, but returning to

California without something permanent and irrevocable between them would be even riskier.

"We should get married." He said it flatly with no elaboration or subtlety.

"Of course," she breathed. "I want to marry you." She stepped toward him and slipped her arms around his waist.

Reeve held her, feeling her warmth and sweetness fill his arms. "I mean now," he said. "Tonight or tomorrow at the latest. Right away."

He could feel Clea stiffen with surprise. "Here in Mexico?" she asked.

"Yes."

Clea tried to hide her confusion. This wasn't the way she'd planned it. She loved Reeve, and she wanted to spend her life with him, but his suggestion had a hint of desperation about it that she didn't like. It was as if he didn't trust her.

Clea turned away and looked out to sea. The moonlight cast a narrow beam across the water. She stared at it for a long time. "I don't understand," she said finally, almost to herself.

"If we go back to Los Angeles without a commitment, it's not going to work, Clea. I remember how it was before, and I can see that happening again. Your family interfering, your career..."

"I don't believe you're saying any of this," she responded. "How can you condemn us without a chance? Of course we can work things out in L.A. We're very different people from the kids we were."

Reeve's next words were painfully honest. "That's right. We're not those idealistic kids who think love can conquer all. We've learned it can't. Maybe I'm afraid that if we go back to L.A. and you have a chance to think it over, you'll change your mind about us."

Clea was stunned. "That's ridiculous! You're acting as if I don't know what I want. Of course, I do, I—"

"Then prove it," he challenged. "Marry me. Stay here with me."

"Prove it?" she repeated. "Why must I prove my love to you? I've been operating on trust, which you seem to have ignored." Reeve was making nonsensical demands on her, and Clea couldn't understand what was the matter with him.

"Maybe you're right," he said. "Maybe I don't trust the future, and that's why I want to grab what I have, here and now."

"Marriage doesn't automatically bring trust, Reeve. A piece of paper means nothing without the commitment—"

"Commitment?" he repeated. "I'm ready for that now. I'm ready to grab onto what I have."

Clea sank down on the bench. The sense of peace had disappeared; she felt very much alone. "You want everything on your terms, Reeve, while I only want some time to plan our lives and adjust to all the changes."

Reeve's response was angry. "You're scared, aren't you? Afraid of going through with it. Daydreaming and fantasizing about our lives together is one thing, but now in the real world—"

"Real world?" Clea shot back. "Is that how you see your life on the *Argosy*, sailing away to never-never land? That isn't real, Reeve."

"I suppose your life is—taking photographs of the rich and famous while you turn your back on your talent."

He was taunting her, Clea thought, wanting her to become angry.

And he was getting just what he wanted. She could feel her heart constricting, and deep in the pit of her stomach was a terrible ache.

Everything that had been so beautiful for them was suddenly ugly; even the square they'd walked into with such happiness only moments before had lost all of its charm. In fact her hopes, her whole world, seemed to be falling apart, and there was nothing Clea could do to stop it.

She leaned back on the bench, feeling the slats cool against her shoulders. They brought her back to reality, and Clea found herself wondering if what Reeve said was true. Maybe she *was* afraid of leaving her safe, secure world in L.A. But Reeve's demand that they marry at once was no solution. In fact, he seemed as scared as she, and the proposal seemed like an act of desperation.

"Well, Clea?"

She felt a threat in his voice, and she answered the only way she knew how. "I love you, Reeve, and I want to be with you, but we have responsibilities at home that we need to take care of—"

"No, Clea," he interrupted. "Our responsibility is to ourselves now, and to no one else."

"What about—"

Once more, he wouldn't let her finish. "Mommie and Daddy and brother Charlie?" Reeve laughed mirthlessly. "Nothing has changed, Clea."

"Why are you doing this to us?" she cried. Tears were starting, and she couldn't control them. "Why are you ripping us apart?"

"It's not just me, Clea." His voice was gentle for the first time. "It's both of us. It's what we are, and that'll never change. I'm committed to you, but you keep backing away, just like last time." He touched her tear-stained face. "I don't think it was ever meant to work out for us, Clea."

She heard the words; her ears rang with them, but still she couldn't believe what was echoing in her head.

Then he spoke again, and it was even worse. "Our adventure is over, Clea, and we need to walk away before we hurt each other more."

So that's what he wanted—to walk away without even trying to work things out. "Time," she said, "just a little time, Reeve."

"We've had ten years, Clea. All the time in the world can't make us into different people no matter how much we want it. Let it go—now, before we cause any more pain."

Before she could recover from his words, the peace of the little square was interrupted. A taxi lumbered down the narrow street and deposited a load of sightseers who headed for the beach, weaving a little from the Mexican beer but obviously enjoying themselves.

"Here's a cab," Reeve said. "Let's get back to the dock so you can call the airlines. I imagine there's time to get a flight out tonight."

Clea looked up at him, but he'd already taken a step toward the waiting cab. As if in shock, she followed him. Her mind seemed incapable of functioning, and she couldn't find the words to say what was inside. Was he right? Was it too late to rewrite the past? Was it all a fantasy of what could never be? All the questions brought back a rush of old fears, which engulfed Clea and left her powerless.

Reeve opened the taxi door, his face withdrawn and stern. Still numb, Clea climbed in. Why was this happening? Her mind screamed out the question, but there was no answer, no way to get through the impenetrable wall he'd built around himself.

They rode to the boat in silence, Reeve not daring to look at Clea for fear of seeing the anger on her face, the hurt. He'd known the risk from the beginning, but still he'd taken the chance. He'd had to make her choose. There'd be no other way. Now the worst had happened, and he'd lost her.

Reeve tried to convince himself that it was better this way, quick as a surgeon's knife, sparing both of them the torment of a slow, painful ending in L.A., an ending they both knew was inevitable.

He'd asked her to marry him ten years ago. Tonight he'd asked again. There wouldn't be a third time.

CLEA PULLED the contact sheets from the line and turned on the light in her darkroom. She didn't have to get out her loop to look at the proofs; she knew they weren't as good as she'd hoped. The composition was all right, but there was no heart in the shots, no soul, as there'd been in the photos she'd gotten in Mexico and Colorado.

As she was taking off her apron, Clea heard the front door open.

"Clea, it's me. Is the red light on?"

"No, Charlie, it's safe. Come on in." She'd picked up a grease pencil and was marking the frames that had possibilities.

"Anything noteworthy?" he asked, slipping into a canvas chair by the darkroom door.

Clea shook her head. "'Fraid not." She didn't want to talk about the reasons for the unsatisfactory pictures, so before her brother had a chance to delve further into the subject Clea asked, "What brings the tycoon to my humble dwellings?" It was easy to get Charlie to talk about himself.

"Not a tycoon yet; that is, I'm still slightly rebellious. Notice that I wear no tie."

"Does Dad approve of that?"

"Nope, but we've compromised. I've done such a good job of running employee relations at Moore Industries the past couple of months, he overlooks my idiosyncrasies."

"It's hard to believe you're back in the fold," Clea said, tossing aside the pencil and plopping down on a stool near Charlie.

"Is it possible that you forgot about my degree in business administration?"

Clea laughed. "I do seem to have a vague memory of that."

"It's true I never chose to use it. Coffee?" he asked, interrupting himself.

Clea nodded toward a pot she always kept perking in the studio and followed Charlie into the larger room where he poured himself a cup.

"How about you?" he asked.

"I don't have a business degree," Clea replied.

"No, Sis, I was asking if you wanted a cup of coffee."

Clea shook her head, laughing.

"Talk about being in left field, Sis. You're really out of it recently."

"I believe we were discussing your business degree," Clea insisted, getting her brother back on track.

"Oh, yes. Well, I never had the occasion to use it until I got the hell scared out of me in Mexico and decided to seek an honest career. As it turns out, I have a flair for working with people. I'm a pretty damned good manager," he said proudly.

"So Dad says. Of course, he gripes that your techniques are a little unorthodox."

"So, he put up a fuss about the day-care center," Charlie said, taking a sip of his coffee. "But I hung in there, and it's going to work. I've learned that it's important to stick by your beliefs with him, just keep on keeping on. Actually Dad—and even Mom—can be reasonable. Maybe they've mellowed."

"Or we've worn them down."

"What's that?" Charlie asked.

"What?" Clea followed his glance to a stack of magazine tear sheets on the desk. "Oh, it's the stuff I did in Colorado."

"Let me see," Charlie insisted.

Reluctantly, Clea handed him the proofs, which Charlie studied carefully. "This is good," he said. "Really nice work, and another world from the *Trends* stuff."

"Yes, *New World* is a good magazine."

"I'm not talking about the magazine, Clea. I'm talking about the pictures. This is some of the best work you've ever done. Keep it up and you'll be ready for a one-woman show."

"Actually," Clea admitted, "I've been approached to do one—"

"Great!"

"—but I really don't have enough work," Clea finished. "They're willing to give me a slot next year if I can come up with some good stuff, but—" Clea glanced toward the darkroom. "I'm having trouble," she admitted.

"Why, Clea?" Charlie prodded.

This was what she'd tried to avoid, but she couldn't go on avoiding it, Clea realized. "My inspiration seems to be lacking." Clea fingered a mounted shot she'd taken in Mexico the afternoon she'd walked through the streets with Reeve.

"He's not back yet," Charlie said.

Clea shot her brother a questioning look.

"Apparently Reeve picked up a cruise in Mexico that kept him busy for a couple of weeks," Charlie explained, "and then he stopped in San Diego and got another booking there."

"Well, I knew he wasn't back, but you certainly know the details."

"I keep in touch," Charlie replied. "By the way, how'd you know he wasn't back?"

"Oh . . ."

"Clea?" Charlie insisted.

"I'm not sure I want to talk about it."

"You have to talk to somebody, some time. Reeve's my best friend, and you're my sister. Who better than old Charlie to tell your troubles to?" He got up and went over to Clea, putting his hand on her shoulder. "What'dya do, drive down to Newport?"

Clea nodded.

"What were you planning to do when you saw him?"

"I'm still trying to figure that out. Tell him the truth, I suppose."

"Which is?"

"I love him, Charlie."

"I know that, so I imagine he does, too," Charlie commented wisely.

"Yes, but I was afraid of that love when we were in Mexico. Reeve wanted a total commitment, but I wanted to please Mom and Dad, do things the right way—my way—and I wanted to hold on to my career."

"So how's that changed?" Charlie asked, leaning against the desk and looking at his sister.

"Even though I was wrong about some things," she admitted, "I was right about others. I did need time."

"And now that you've had six weeks of time?"

"It didn't take that long for me to see that I wasn't happy photographing life-styles of the rich and boring. I wanted to spread my wings a little, take some chances, maybe even dare to fail."

"But you didn't fail. Selling the story about Miss Etta proved you have the talent to break into the journalistic market in a big way."

"That was a great boost to my morale," Clea admitted, "just the push I needed to keep on trying."

"So what do Mom and Dad say about it all?"

Clea laughed. "Mom misses being my unofficial booking agent, and she has a long list of disappointed friends, but she and Dad are proud. They understand that only I can make choices about my future."

"You ignored an important part of the question, Sis. What did they say about it *all?*"

"Meaning Reeve?"

"Meaning Reeve. Come on, this is like pulling teeth. How much did you tell them?"

"Everything." She grinned. "Well, almost everything. I told them about Mexico and Denver, and I told them I was still in love with Reeve."

"Glad I wasn't around for the fireworks."

"Their reaction ran the gamut from surprise to disbelief to consternation and finally fear."

"Fear? Not Dad, surely."

"I'm serious," Clea affirmed. "I think Mom—and Dad—have both been afraid for years that Reeve would somehow steal me away. But if I get him back, I mean *when* I get him back, I won't be choosing between my parents and the man I love. There's room in my heart for everyone. It's just that none of us understood that before."

Charlie whistled appreciatively. "You sound very levelheaded and together, Clea. I'm impressed."

"Maybe I'm too levelheaded. I should have taken a chance with Reeve in Mexico."

Charlie leaned over and gave her a hug. "Being levelheaded isn't so bad, which I must say is a weird remark coming from me. But you've had time to work things through, and you've made tremendous changes in your life these past weeks. You know what you want."

"Yes, but can I get it?" Clea asked.

"My money's on you, kid."

"SO HOW DOES IT FEEL to be back in home port? Long time no see." Pokey Barstow leaned both elbows on the counter, ready to settle in for a long chat.

"Great," Reeve said, "if only I could stay in port. I docked this morning, and I'm heading out again tonight. My agent booked me for some damned honeymoon cruise."

"Lovebirds, eh?" Pokey rolled his eyes expressively.

"Just what I need." Reeve almost growled the words as he pushed his empty plate away.

"So get out of it," Pokey suggested.

"I tried. Seems they paid up front and he can't reach them. Apparently, the happy couple is on the way to Newport." He glanced at his watch and moaned. "They'll be here any time."

"Some people would like the steady work," Pokey reminded him.

"I have things to do here," Reeve said vaguely.

"Like?"

"Looks like a customer wants you down at the end of the counter," Reeve said.

Pokey took off reluctantly, and Reeve breathed a sigh of relief. He didn't feel like going into his personal life with Pokey tonight.

During the past few weeks his thoughts had revolved around Clea, and she was still the only thing on his mind. What a fool he'd been to demand that she marry him on the spot. He'd been so damned afraid of losing her that he'd ended up scaring her away.

"Self-fulfilling prophecy," he murmured aloud.

She'd been right about needing time, but he'd been afraid to believe in her or in himself. He'd demanded that she walk away from her career, her family, her friends, without even a backward glance. When she'd hesitated, he'd jumped to the worst possible conclusion.

And what had he offered to give up? Nothing. Oh, he'd talked a lot about commitment, but he'd said nothing about compromise. That would change. He couldn't make it without Clea, and he'd do whatever necessary to get her back. Reeve hoped it wasn't too late.

He went to the end of the bar and handed Pokey a dollar. "Change for the pay phone, please, Poke."

"Use mine," Pokey answered. "It's for friends."

Reeve dialed Clea's number. After three rings the answering machine picked up. Inwardly he cursed. This wasn't the way he'd meant to do it, but he had no choice.

"Clea, it's Reeve. I need to talk to you, but I have to go out on a charter in a few hours." He took a deep breath and tried to organize his thoughts.

"You were right. We needed time to talk about our future and make plans. I guess I was too damned scared of losing you to listen to you. I'm ready to listen now, and I'm ready to compromise. I want you to have your career, and I want you to please your parents. Hell, I'll even take them on a cruise."

There was so much to say, but he knew the tape would cut him off, so Reeve got right to the point. "Will you marry me?" he asked.

"I know. I said I wouldn't ask again, but maybe the third time's a charm. Please be here for me when I get back."

Reeve hung up and turned to find Pokey's bright eyes on him.

"Just business," he lied, pulling out his wallet to pay for dinner.

"On the house tonight, Captain," Pokey said. "Sounds like you need a friend."

Reeve mustered a smile of thanks and went outside. It was in Clea's hands now, and he could only hope she'd missed him as much as he'd missed her.

As he walked through the twilight toward the marina, he wondered why his agent had scheduled a charter tonight. He'd have to tell them that he and his crew wouldn't be ready to sail until dawn. Maybe he could talk them into going to a motel. Reeve really didn't want any company tonight, especially not honeymooners.

As he stepped on board, he noted a pile of luggage on the deck. Down below he could see a light in the main cabin. They were certainly making themselves at home, Reeve thought irritably as he strode down the companionway and pushed open the door to his cabin.

"Excuse me, but—"

His passenger turned to greet him. "No excuses this time, Reeve."

"Clea," he whispered, his heart in his throat. "I was expecting a charter . . ."

"It's me," she said almost defiantly. "I'm booked and paid for, and you can't get rid of me." Her face was serious, and in her brown eyes was the most determined look Reeve had ever seen.

"Get rid of you? Clea, I—"

She interrupted him. "Listen to me, Reeve, please, and don't stop me until I finish because if you do, I might never finish."

Clea knew she wasn't making much sense, but she'd gotten a good look at him, which had interrupted her train of thought.

He looked wonderful, his face bronzed from the sun, his hair damp with the sea air, his muscular body taut with tension and expectation. Never had she loved him as much as at this moment. If she could just convince him of it. She took a deep breath.

"You were right. I was afraid in Mexico, afraid of losing my old life. When I got back here and started looking at myself and that life I didn't want to lose, none of it seemed important. In fact, I didn't like my career or what it had turned me into."

Reeve spoke up then. "You needed time to figure that out for yourself; instead I tried to tell you how to feel and think."

"Yes, you did," Clea agreed.

That stopped Reeve for a moment; then he laughed.

"And thank heavens I figured it out. I know who I am and what I want. I'm at my best around you, Reeve. I do my best work when you're with me. I can't make it as a person or a professional without you."

In two long strides he was across the room, holding her, kissing her, feeling her tears of joy against his own damp cheeks.

"Tell me what you want," he murmured between kisses. "I can give up the boat, settle down."

"Don't you dare." She touched his face with her fingertips. "This is your life, and I need to share it with you as my best friend, my lover and my inspiration. Besides," she added with a twinkle, "I'm counting on you to take me to more wonderful places so I can accumulate work for my show."

"What show?" he questioned.

"I'll tell you later, but first we have to make an honest man of you and turn this into a real honeymoon cruise. You've asked me twice so now it's my turn. Will you marry me, Reeve Holden?"

Reeve felt a great surge of happiness sweep through him. Somehow, they'd made it. He hugged her with all his might. "You bet I'll marry you." Reeve laughed to himself, thinking of his message on the answering machine.

"Tonight?" she insisted.

"Nope," he replied. "We're going to wait until we get to Santa Inez then fly Charlie and your parents down for a huge fiesta. We deserve it."

Clea kissed him again, deeply, hungrily, not really believing that she was in his arms. She raised her eyes to his, speaking the word from long ago that had deeper meaning than ever before. "I'll never love another man."

His eyes promised a lifetime. "I'll love you forever, Clea."

They kissed again and clung to each other, hearts filled with joy. Reeve nuzzled her lovingly. "You've never slept in the captain's bed, have you?"

Clea looked up at him, her eyes teasing. "Last time I was crew, remember?"

"That reminds me. I need to cancel my crew for tomorrow. That is, if you think we can handle the *Argosy* on our own."

"I don't have the slightest doubt, Captain."

Reeve took her hand and pulled her toward the door. Then he stopped, remembering the earlier question. "What's this about a show?"

"Oh, just my one-woman show, that's all," she bragged. "I guess you don't know about the reaction to my magazine piece on Miss Etta, do you?"

"I didn't even know it was a magazine piece. Guess I have a lot to catch up on."

Clea took his arm firmly as they stepped onto the companionway. "We have plenty of time, my darling. The rest of our lives."

With a laugh Reeve swept her into his arms and kicked open the door to his cabin. "Who says happy endings are only in books?"

From the author of
DADDY, DARLING

DOCTOR, DARLING
by
Glenda Sanders

The eagerly awaited sequel to DADDY,
DARLING is here! In DOCTOR, DARLING,
the imposing Dr. Sergei Karol meets his match.
He's head over heels in love with Polly
Mechler, the adorable TV celebrity whose
plumbing-supply commercials have made her
a household name. But Sergei wants Polly to
be adorable just for him . . . and Polly isn't one
to follow doctor's orders!

**Watch for DOCTOR, DARLING.
Coming in January 1991**

TDDR

History is now twice as exciting, twice as romantic!

Harlequin is proud to announce that, by popular demand, Harlequin Historicals will be increasing from two to four titles per month, starting in February 1991.

Even if you've never read a historical romance before, you will love the great stories you've come to expect from favorite authors like Patricia Potter, Lucy Elliot, Ruth Langan and Heather Graham Pozzessere.

Enter the world of Harlequin Historicals and share the adventures of cowboys and captains, pirates and princes.

*Available wherever
Harlequin books are sold.*

Take 4 bestselling love stories FREE

Plus get a FREE surprise gift!

H A R L E Q U I N

American Romance®

RELIVE THE MEMORIES....

From New York's immigrant experience to San Francisco's Great Quake of '06. From the western front of World War I to the Roaring Twenties. From the indomitable spirit of the thirties to the home front of the Fabulous Forties to the baby-boom fifties...A CENTURY OF AMERICAN ROMANCE takes you on a nostalgic journey.

From the turn of the century to the dawn of the year 2000, you'll revel in the romance of a time gone by and sneak a peek at romance in an exciting future.

Watch for all the CENTURY OF AMERICAN ROMANCE titles coming to you one per month over the next four months in Harlequin American Romance.

Don't miss a day of A CENTURY OF AMERICAN ROMANCE.

A CENTURY OF
AMERICAN ROMANCE
1960s

The women...the men...the passions...the memories...

Harlequin romances are now available in stores at these convenient times each month.

Harlequin Presents
Harlequin American Romance
Harlequin Historical
Harlequin Intrigue

These series will be in stores on the 4th of every month.

Harlequin Romance
Harlequin Temptation
Harlequin Superromance
Harlequin Regency Romance

New titles for these series will be in stores on the 16th of every month.

We hope this new schedule is convenient for you. With only two trips each month to your local bookseller, you will always be sure not to miss any of your favorite authors!

Happy reading!

Please note there may be slight variations in on-sale dates in your area due to differences in shipping and handling.

HDATES